Arthur W. Pinero

The Weaker Sex

A Comedy in Three Acts

Arthur W. Pinero

The Weaker Sex
A Comedy in Three Acts

ISBN/EAN: 9783744783347

Printed in Europe, USA, Canada, Australia, Japan

Cover: Foto ©Andreas Hilbeck / pixelio.de

More available books at **www.hansebooks.com**

THE WEAKER SEX

A COMEDY IN THREE ACTS

BY

ARTHUR W. PINERO

BOSTON

1894

THE FIRST ACT

RIGHTS AND WRONGS

At Mrs. Boyle-Chewton's ; Regent's Park.

THE SECOND ACT

THE LOVE THAT LIVES

At Lord Gillingham's ; Kensington.

THE THIRD ACT

MOTHER AND DAUGHTER

At Mrs. Boyle-Chewton's again.

THE PERSONS OF THE PLAY.

IRA LEE.

LADY VIVASH.

SYLVIA (her daughter).

DUDLEY SILCHESTER.

MRS. BOYLE-CHEWTON.

RHODA (her daughter).

MR. BARGUS, M.P.

LORD GILLINGHAM.

LADY GILLINGHAM.

LADY LIPTROTT.

HON. GEORGE LIPTROTT.

MR. HAWLEY HILL.

MRS. HAWLEY HILL.

MR. WADE GREEN.

PETCH (servant at Mrs. Boyle-Chewton's).

SPENCER (servant at Lord Gillingham's).

INTRODUCTORY NOTE

ALTHOUGH "The Weaker Sex" was produced in London but a month before "The Profligate" first saw the light, and just a year after "Sweet Lavender," it really belongs to an earlier period of Mr. Pinero's work; indeed, its composition may be said to date between "Lords and Commons" and the Court series of farces. It was this play, as I have stated elsewhere, that Mr. Pinero offered to Mr. John Clayton and Mr. Arthur Cecil when in the winter of 1884 they appealed to him in their sore need for a piece, their management of the Court being at that time in anything but a flourishing condition; and it was only Mr. Clayton's uncertainty about "The Weaker Sex" that led to Mr. Pinero offering "The Magistrate" in its place, a turn of events which proved most fortunate for the Court management. Meanwhile, "The Weaker Sex" was laid by for about four years, when Mr. and Mrs. Kendal secured the rights of the play, and produced it tentatively at the Theatre Royal, Manchester, on September 28, 1888. The result was so encouraging that when, after their tour, Mr. and Mrs. Kendal arranged with Mrs.

5

John Wood to take the new Court Theatre for a season in the spring of 1889, they signalized their reappearance in town by the production of Mr. Pinero's comedy. It was on Saturday, March 16, 1889, that this play was first seen in London, but it must be noted that it was not presented here exactly as it had been in Manchester; for after the provincial trial Mr. Pinero abolished the conventional "happy ending" he had originally contrived, which was found to be unsatisfactory, and printed the play as it is now printed.

The following is a copy of the " first night " programme at the Court Theatre, London: —

ROYAL COURT THEATRE.

UNDER THE MANAGEMENT OF MRS. JOHN WOOD.

APPEARANCE OF MR. AND MRS. KENDAL.

ON SATURDAY, MARCH 16, AT 8.30,

AND EVERY EVENING,

Will be Performed an Original Modern Play in Three Acts,
Entitled

THE WEAKER SEX,

BY

A. W. PINERO.

LORD GILLINGHAM . .	Mr. A. W. DENISON.
HON. GEORGE LIPTROTT .	Mr. E. ALLAN AYNESWORTH.
MR. BARGUS, M. P. . .	Mr. EDWARD RIGHTON.
CAPTAIN JESSETT . . .	Mr. A. B. FRANCIS.
DUDLEY SILCHESTER . .	Mr. W. H. VERNON.
IRA LEE	Mr. KENDAL.
MR. HAWLEY HILL . .	Mr. W. NEWALL.
MR. WADE GREEN . .	Mr. ERIC LEWIS.
SPENCER (servant at Lord Gillingham's) . . .	Mr. H. DEANE.
LADY GILLINGHAM . .	Miss VIOLET VANBRUGH.
LADY LIPTROTT . . .	Miss PATTY CHAPMAN.
LADY STRUDDOCK . . .	Miss E. MATHEWS.

LADY VIVASH . . . . Mrs. KENDAL.
SYLVIA (her daughter) . Miss ANNIE HUGHES.
MRS. HAWLEY HILL . . Miss TREVOR BISHOP.
MRS. BOYLE-CHEWTON . Miss FANNY COLEMAN.
RHODA (her daughter) . Miss OLGA BRANDON.
MISS CARDELLOE . . . Miss BLANCHE ELLICE.
PETCH (servant at Mrs.
   Boyle-Chewton's) . . Miss C. LUCIE.

ACT I.

RIGHTS AND WRONGS.

At Mrs. Boyle-Chewton's, Regent's Park.

ACT II.

THE LOVE THAT LIVES.

At Lord Gillingham's, Kensington.

ACT III.

MOTHER AND DAUGHTER.

At Mrs. Boyle-Chewton's again.

THE NEW SCENERY BY MR. THOMAS W. HALL.

The success achieved in London was fair, though not great, and after a satisfactory run of some weeks the play was withdrawn; but on their provincial tours Mr. and Mrs. Kendal have always found "The Weaker Sex" received with marked favor, while in America they have played it continuously with very great success, and it still holds its own.

MALCOLM C. SALAMAN.

September, 1894.

THE WEAKER SEX

THE FIRST ACT

The scene is the library in MRS. BOYLE-CHEWTON'S *house in Sussex Gardens, Regent's Park, the windows opening on to the garden, and giving a view of the ornamental water beyond. The room is handsomely but rather gloomily furnished, and books and newspapers are scattered everywhere, the whole place wearing a busy aspect. On one wall is a large printed poster, as follows : —*

UNION OF INDEPENDENT WOMEN.

———

A GREAT PUBLIC MEETING
Under the auspices of the Union, will be held at the

ST. SIMON'S HALL, PICCADILLY,

ON MONDAY, MAY 5TH,

Having for its Object a Demonstrative Assertion of
the Rights of Women to share the Privileges
and Penalties of the other Sex in
all Spheres of Life.

11

The Chair will be taken at 8 o'clock by

Mrs. E. BOYLE-CHEWTON, M.L.S.B.

The following Speakers will address the Meeting: —

LADY VIVASH ;

Miss Anna W. Perkyn, from Montreal; Mrs. McOstrich;
Miss Awke; Mrs. Clymper-Boosby; and

MR. BARGUS,

M.P. for Skipping-Molton,

Who will take this opportunity to declare his
adherence to

A MIGHTY AND IRRESISTIBLE MOVEMENT.

All are invited!

Women! bring Decent, Rational Thinking Men.

No INFANTS.

MRS. BOYLE-CHEWTON, *a woman of about forty,
with a not unpleasing face, but a rigid person-
ality, her hair worn straight and short, and her
costume severe, dowdy, and ungainly, sits writing at one end of a writing-table ; while at the
other her daughter* RHODA, *a pretty girl of
about nineteen, dressed in the same fashion,
dozes with a pen in her hand, but hidden from
her mother by the stationery cabinet.*

MRS. BOYLE-CHEWTON.

[*Taking up the letter she has been writing and
surveying it critically.*] I think I make myself
understood. Listen, Rhoda. I have thought it
expedient to adapt myself to this pugilistic person's phraseology. [*Reading.*] "Mrs. E. Boyle-
Chewton accepts the offer of Mr. Robert Saunders
of Endell Street, Bloomsbury, to supply her with
four 'chuckers-out' for the great meeting to-night
at the St. Simon's Hall." A chucker-out, my dear
Rhoda, is Mr. Saunders's definition of a person
who ejects disorderly characters. [*Resuming.*]
"Mrs. Boyle-Chewton does not think 'five shillings
a nob' at all exorbitant, but must decline the prof-
fered services of *Mrs.* Robert Saunders; for while
fully grasping Mr. Saunders's assurance that his
wife is upon a physical equality with 'ten men and
a boy,' Mrs. Boyle-Chewton doubts whether this
particular branch of enterprise should be included
in woman's furthest ambitions." Um — yes —
that provides for any fractious opposition, I think.
[*Enclosing and addressing the letter.*] Have you

copied the plan of to-night's proceedings? [*Impatiently.*] Rhoda! [*Discovering that* RHODA *is asleep.*] Good gracious! Rhoda, you're asleep.

RHODA.

[*Waking with a start.*] Oh! I — I must have closed my eyes.

MRS. BOYLE-CHEWTON.

I am ashamed of you!

RHODA.

I beg your pardon, mamma. It is the heat, I think.

MRS. BOYLE-CHEWTON.

Heat! It will be hotter at the meeting! You've no enthusiasm!

RHODA.

I have been sitting since eight o'clock this morning. I gobbled my breakfast. [*Thumping her chest.*] I can feel it here now.

MRS. BOYLE-CHEWTON.

I'm not surprised — you had four cutlets. *I* have been sitting upon two eggs.

RHODA.

[*Giving* MRS. BOYLE-CHEWTON *a paper.*] There, the plans are finished.

PETCH, *a middle-aged woman-servant, grim and shapeless, enters the room.*

Petch.

Mr. Silchester!

Mrs. Boyle-Chewton.

[*Impatiently.*]   Oh, dear! oh, dear!

Dudley Silchester, *a fashionably dressed handsome-bearded man of about forty, enters breezily.*

Dudley.

[*Kissing* Mrs. Boyle-Chewton.]   Good-morning, Edith.

Mrs. Boyle-Chewton.

Good-morning, brother Dudley.

Dudley.

[*Kissing* Rhoda.]   Well, Rhoda dear?

Rhoda.

Well, Uncle Dud?

Mrs. Boyle-Chewton.

[*Giving letter and plan to* Petch.]   That letter by cab to Endell Street.   Lay the paper on the Committee Room table.   [Petch *goes out.*

Dudley.

[*To* Rhoda.]   You look tired.

Rhoda.

Hush!

Mrs. Boyle-Chewton.

I dare say we *all* look tired, Dudley.   You know what to-night is ?

Dudley.

I think — Monday night.

Mrs. Boyle-Chewton.

[*Waving her hand towards the bill.*] The night of our great meeting.

Dudley.

[*Looking at the bill.*] Oh, yes, of course, our great meeting.   Sorry an old engagement to play whist at the club will prevent my— It suggests the circus.

Mrs. Boyle-Chewton.

I call those names.

Dudley.

Yes — I dare say other people will call them names in the course of the evening.

Mrs. Boyle-Chewton.

It will be a monster meeting.

Dudley.

What's that — meeting of monsters ?

Mrs. Boyle-Chewton.

Dudley !   If you come to my house merely to —

DUDLEY.

Beg pardon, Edith. [*Producing a letter.*] I dropped in to show you this.

MRS. BOYLE-CHEWTON.

[*Opening the letter.*] Rhoda, your uncle is offered the appointment of Consul at Palermo! What a very excellent thing! Through whom?

DUDLEY.

Lord Gillingham, I fancy.

MRS. BOYLE-CHEWTON.

Ah, Lady Vivash, dear Mary, must have gained his influence for you.

RHODA.

Oh, I'm so glad, Uncle Dud — and so sorry !

MRS. BOYLE-CHEWTON.

£600 a year — that's more than your services are worth, Dudley.

DUDLEY.

Yes — or ever will be.

MRS. BOYLE-CHEWTON.

Why, you're surely not going to —

DUDLEY.

Accept it ? Certainly not.

MRS. BOYLE-CHEWTON.

Refuse it! When you've never done a real stroke of work in your life.

DUDLEY.

Never had anybody to work for.

MRS. BOYLE-CHEWTON.

You've had yourself.

DUDLEY.

Oh, everybody's had *me* at one time or another. I don't reckon myself.

MRS. BOYLE-CHEWTON.

The epitaph of every wasted career. Why *not* go to Palermo?

DUDLEY.

Can't get away just now.

MRS. BOYLE-CHEWTON.

You've nothing to do in London.

DUDLEY.

That's it — if I had I should be glad to go to Palermo.

MRS. BOYLE-CHEWTON.

I know. I can read you like a book, brother Dudley.

DUDLEY.

I'm sure you can, sister Edith. The intelligent world has read me like a book at least for the last quarter of a century. It has read me, thumbed me, cut me, — ah, yes, cut me, — and made brutal marginal notes upon me, until I am the soiled, dog-eared volume so out of keeping with your immaculate library.

MRS. BOYLE-CHEWTON.

Rhoda, leave me with your uncle for a few moments.

RHODA.

Yes, mamma.

DUDLEY.

Have mercy, Edith. [*To* RHODA.] Keep within earshot in case I shriek for assistance.

> [RHODA *goes out into the garden, where for a while she is seen at intervals walking to and fro reading.*]

MRS. BOYLE-CHEWTON.

Dudley, you will decline to go to Palermo because you are still hankering after your old sweetheart, Lady Vivash. If I'm wrong say No. [DUDLEY *reflects for a moment, smilingly looks at* MRS. BOYLE-CHEWTON, *and then without a word drops into an arm-chair.*] Ah, I thought so! Dudley, of all the extravagant, hopeless passions man ever had for woman, your attachment to my old school-fellow and present colleague, Mary Vivash, is the most senseless my mind can grasp!

DUDLEY.

My dear Edith, a respectful affection, which commenced on my side for your schoolmate, Mary Norbury, as she then was, about twenty years ago, is hardly deserving of such severe stricture. It has at least the merit of antiquity; give it as much respect as you would afford an Anglo-Roman tumulus or an ancient Greek coin.

MRS. BOYLE-CHEWTON.

It began most absurdly.

DUDLEY.

It began by my bringing English toffee to the little *pension* at Bruges, where you were monitress, and Mary Norbury, a child of fifteen, was fourth scholar.

MRS. BOYLE-CHEWTON.

I thought it was ridiculous *then!*

DUDLEY.

You took your share of the toffee; and, oh, what toffee! Life has given me since nothing so sweet as that cooked sugar we portioned out twenty years ago on the side-paths of those old canals.

MRS. BOYLE-CHEWTON.

And then, Dudley, after all —

DUDLEY.

All that toffee — tons of it.

MRS. BOYLE-CHEWTON.

After all — she refused you!

DUDLEY.

Um — in favor of a brighter, better, cleverer fellow — my friend, Philip Lyster.

MRS. BOYLE-CHEWTON.

And Philip Lyster she quarrelled with — marrying old Lord Vivash a month afterwards in a fit of mad rage.

DUDLEY.

He's gone — thank goodness!

MRS. BOYLE-CHEWTON.

Yes; and she's had enough of marriage to last her a lifetime.

DUDLEY.

She hasn't told me that.

MRS. BOYLE-CHEWTON.

My dear brother, even if she *did* think of marrying again, her mind would go back — to whom do you imagine?

DUDLEY.

I thought perhaps to —

MRS. BOYLE-CHEWTON.

To *you!* Fiddlesticks! To her only real love, Philip Lyster, whose heart she broke.

DUDLEY.

Where *is* he ? In heaven, for all we know.

MRS. BOYLE-CHEWTON.

Nonsense, you men don't go there so surely. You see, my dear Dudley, you haven't a ghost of a chance. Besides, your conduct is cruel to *me*.

DUDLEY.

My dear Edith !

MRS. BOYLE-CHEWTON.

You know what I have at heart, — the Advance- ment of Women from the Rear to the Van !

DUDLEY.

[*Nervously putting on his gloves.*] Yes — I think, Edith, you've before explained —

MRS. BOYLE-CHEWTON.

Our recruit, Lady Vivash, supplies the impetus this great movement requires. She is now a strong, self-reliant, fine-minded creature.

DUDLEY.

She is.

MRS. BOYLE-CHEWTON.

She is still young, brilliant, and enthusiastic —

DUDLEY.

That's true !

MRS. BOYLE-CHEWTON.

With beauty and a title — which oughtn't to count, but it does!

DUDLEY.

I should think so.

MRS. BOYLE-CHEWTON.

Since she has thrown her soul in with us we have not only doubled our women supporters, but we are securing fickle, fluctuating, flabby men!

DUDLEY.

Are you!

MRS. BOYLE-CHEWTON.

And now when she has taken up her abode under my roof, and is a necessity to our cause, to see you idling here — nursing your old affection like a dilettante with a cracked china jar! — it must be most distracting to her, as it is annoying to me.

DUDLEY.

Cracked jar! You are right, it *is* cracked! only the scent of the roses or the smell of the ginger, or whatever was in it, will linger — dash it! it will linger.

LADY VIVASH, *a beautiful woman of about thirty-five, dressed with the most rigid simplicity, but without any sacrifice of grace or dignity, enters quickly from the garden.*

LADY VIVASH.

At what time is the committee, dear? [*Giving her hand pleasantly to* DUDLEY.] How do you do, Mr. Silchester? We are gloriously busy. You have come to scoff, of course.

MRS. BOYLE-CHEWTON.

Committee at one; there's half an hour yet.

LADY VIVASH.

Have any of our ladies arrived?

DUDLEY.

I think so.

LADY VIVASH.

Indeed?

DUDLEY.

I saw some goloshes in the hall as I came in.

LADY VIVASH.

I wear goloshes in the damp weather. Perhaps they are mine.

DUDLEY.

Perhaps; I didn't know at first *whether* they were goloshes.

LADY VIVASH.

What did you take them for?

DUDLEY.

Gondolas.

LADY VIVASH.

Oh! [*Writing busily.*] After all, the size of a woman's foot is quite immaterial. A woman doesn't carry her heart in her boots.

DUDLEY.

She does — if you say " Boo ! " in the dark.

LADY VIVASH.

That's your opinion of women — not mine.

DUDLEY.

Because you're not a man.

LADY VIVASH.

I wish I were for a month.

DUDLEY.

I dare say you do — a jolly month you'd have of it !

MRS. BOYLE-CHEWTON.

Dudley !

DUDLEY.

What I mean, my dear Edith, is that a month would enable dear Lady Vivash to taste the sweets and not the bitters of manhood ; to wrench, as it were, the door-knocker of adolescence without paying the forty shillings of maturity. I have been a grown man for twenty years out of my forty, and the result is that I wish sincerely —

LADY VIVASH.

You wish you had been born a woman!

DUDLEY.

No; a quadruped. A beast is short-lived.

PETCH *enters.*

PETCH.

Mr. Bargus is in the Committee Room.

MRS. BOYLE-CHEWTON.

Oh, here's Mr. Bargus! Dudley, how fortunate you are! — you shall make his acquaintance. [*To* PETCH.] Ask Mr. Bargus to come here.

[PETCH *goes out.*

DUDLEY.

Bargus! Who's Bargus?

MRS. BOYLE-CHEWTON.

You don't read your parliamentary reports, Dudley.

DUDLEY.

Never.

MRS. BOYLE-CHEWTON.

Mr. Bargus is the new member for the Skipping-Molton Division of Cuddleford. We have secured him.

DUDLEY.

Secured him? Is he a very violent M.P. ?

Mrs. Boyle-Chewton.

He is young — as a politician, a mere infant.
We have undertaken, as it were, to nurse him —
to form his ideas.

Dudley.

Kind of political baby-farmers.

Lady Vivash.

As you please. We women need help in the
House.

Dudley.

Wouldn't a charwoman —

Lady Vivash.

In the House of Commons. We want a lever to
raise the mountain of prejudice. We looked about
us, and our eye rested upon — upon —

Mrs. Boyle-Chewton.

The member for the Skipping-Molton Division
of Cuddleford.

Rhoda *enters quickly, thinking* Dudley *is alone.*

Rhoda.

O Uncle Dud, here's that ridiculous little
Bargus!

Mrs. Boyle-Chewton.

Rhoda!

Rhoda.

O mamma!

MRS. BOYLE-CHEWTON.

Ridiculous Bargus! To whom do you allude?

RHODA.

I am afraid I meant Mr. Bargus, mamma; I —
I have taken rather a — not a fancy to Mr. Bargus.

[PETCH *announces* "MR. BARGUS." BAR-
GUS *enters. He is a chubby little gentleman of about forty, with a foolish face
and a large development of forehead, and
his fair hair worn in tight little curls all
over his head, giving him the appearance
of a middle-aged Cupid.*]

MRS. BOYLE-CHEWTÓN.

My dear Mr. Bargus, your name was on our lips.

BARGUS.

Very gratified.

MRS. BOYLE-CHEWTON.

Are you armed for the fray to-night?

BARGUS.

I think so. I rehearsed my speech yesterday to
an invalid cousin with most gratifying results.
Good-morning, Lady Vivash. Good-morning, Miss
Chewton. [*Catching* DUDLEY'S *eye and bowing.*]
An enthusiast, I hope?

LADY VIVASH.

Mr. Silchester — Mr. Clarence Bargus.

DUDLEY.

How d'ye do?

BARGUS.

How d'ye do?

DUDLEY.

You're nervous about to-night — this big meeting, eh? Funkey, just a little?

BARGUS.

It's an ordeal. A friend of mine, interested in women, had two reticules and a vinaigrette thrown at him last week, at Barnchester.

[*Dabbing his brow with his handkerchief.*

LADY VIVASH.

[*To* DUDLEY.] Great head, isn't it?

DUDLEY.

Big head — one of the biggest I've ever seen.

LADY VIVASH.

He's the son of Bargus, the large weaver.

DUDLEY.

Large weaver — that accounts for it.

LADY VIVASH.

Of course he's timid and provincial at present, but he'll float.

DUDLEY.

That head ought to keep him up.　Couldn't you get a more imposing champion ?

LADY VIVASH.

We have others who are — different looking. But Mr. Bargus is all our own.

[*Joins* MRS. BOYLE-CHEWTON *and* BARGUS.

DUDLEY.

Oh, *I* don't want any.　[*To* RHODA.]　So you don't cotton to the political baby, Rhoda ?

RHODA.

No.　You won't say anything if I tell you something funny about him, will you.

DUDLEY.

Honor bright.

RHODA.

Do you know, that when mamma and Lady Vivash are not looking, little Bargus — he — he —

DUDLEY.

Well ?

RHODA.

He does his best to flirt with me.

DUDLEY.

Oh, the forward infant !　I should like to do my best to slap him.

RHODA.

Oh, no; don't. I hate little Bargus, but I'm wretchedly dull here! Nobody ever comes to the house but gentlemanly women and zoölogical-looking men — even Bargus is a relief.

BARGUS.

[*To* LADY VIVASH *and* MRS. BOYLE-CHEWTON.] I have plunged into this great subject of Woman after anxious deliberation. I looked about me in the House, and I saw every man metaphorically waving a banner. One member is for everything — another is against everything. One is for opening everything on a Sunday — another is for closing everything always. I said to myself, " Bargus, what are you going to do to repay the confidence of 8,570 constituents of the Skipping-Molton Division of Cuddleford ? " And in answer came the flapping of wings, and your voices, ladies, saying, " Inscribe the word Woman upon your banner, and march forth ! "

MRS. BOYLE-CHEWTON.

O Mr. Bargus, are you going to say anything like that to-night ?

BARGUS.

[*Dabbing his forehead.*] Well, that's a little bit out of what I *am* going to say to-night.

RHODA.

[*To* DUDLEY, *pointing out of window.*] Why, look at those Gibson girls out there, playing lawn tennis !

Dudley.

They have spotted noses.

Rhoda.

I know — but I envy them the frocks they wear, the partners that feed them with strawberries and cream, the dances, the theatres, everything! They lead girls' lives!

Dudley.

Tush! Your turn will come.

Rhoda.

Will it! What about Lady Vivash's child, Sylvia, who is younger than I, and travelling in Italy with Lady Gillingham? Italy! Fancy! Is *her* turn to *come?* Without ever having seen Sylvia Vivash, I detest her!

Dudley.

Hush! She's a mere child.

Rhoda.

Which I've never been! I've always been a woman with rights! O Uncle Dudley, I've a big right — to be very, very miserable!

Petch *enters.*

Petch.

The committee's here, — Mrs. McOstrich, Mrs. Boosby, and Miss Awke.

MRS. BOYLE-CHEWTON.

Thank you, Petch. Mr. Bargus, pray follow
me. Lady Vivash, please! Rhoda, bring the
minute-book into the Committee Room.

[PETCH *goes out, then* MRS. BOYLE-CHEWTON.
RHODA *is following with an immense
book which she has taken from the writing-table, when* BARGUS *stops her.*]

BARGUS.

Miss Chewton — will you allow me ?

[*Taking the book from her.*

RHODA.

Oh, thank you, Mr. Bargus!

BARGUS.

[*In an undertone.*] May I ask you if you are
fond of flowers, Miss Chewton? If so, I should
much like —

RHODA.

I'm very fond of them; but mamma says wearing flowers is frivolous and unhealthy.

BARGUS.

Oh, then, Miss Chewton, if to-night my speech
happens to develop some trifling little oratorical
blossoms, will you wear them in your memory,
Miss Chewton?

DUDLEY.

[*Watching them.*] H'm! Getting over that nervousness, Mr. Bargus?

BARGUS.

Fairly, sir, thank you.

DUDLEY.

Thought so.

[BARGUS *goes out, followed by* RHODA. LADY VIVASH, *who has been looking into the garden, crosses to the door.*]

LADY VIVASH.

Good-by, Mr. Silchester.

DUDLEY.

Lady Vivash, will you spare me a moment?

LADY VIVASH.

You won't ask me for more, will you?

DUDLEY.

[*Handing her the letter which* MRS. BOYLE-CHEWTON *had read.*] I think I have to thank you for that.

LADY VIVASH.

[*Reading the letter.*] Oh, the offer of the Consulship at Palermo. I am so glad. [*Returning him the letter.*] I did, indeed, suggest to Lord

Gillingham that if he knew of anything that would — that would —

DUDLEY.

That would get an idle, troublesome old friend out of your way —

LADY VIVASH.

I am sorry I have hurt you, Mr. Silchester.

DUDLEY.

You *do* want me to go, then ?

LADY VIVASH.

I think it would be better for you.

DUDLEY.

I couldn't go — alone.

LADY VIVASH.

Isn't Griggs with you still ?

DUDLEY.

My servant ? Yes. But somehow when Griggs has brushed my coat and my hat, and played with my boot-trees for half an hour every morning, there's still a sense of loneliness in life. [*She turns away from him, leaning against the mantelpiece.*] Mary ! Mary !

LADY VIVASH.

[*After a pause.*] Yes.

DUDLEY.

Come with me to Palermo.

LADY VIVASH.

Thank you very much, but your sister Edith and I are so engrossed in our work here that we can't take a holiday just now.

DUDLEY.

It isn't a part of my suggestion that we should disturb Edith.

LADY VIVASH.

I think I must go into the Committee Room.

DUDLEY.

[*Standing before her, clasping his hands.*] Mary, do — *do* marry me. I have waited. I am your oldest friend — make me your newest love. For the sake of your little Sylvia, whom I will cherish as if she were my own, be my wife! For your sake, be my wife! For my sake, be my wife!

LADY VIVASH.

I am very sorry, Dudley, but — I cannot.

DUDLEY.

Cannot give up this life you have chosen? O Mary, what a mistake — what a waste!

LADY VIVASH.

A mistake, perhaps. I may be too weak a woman, mind and body, to fight the great battle

for my sisters. But a waste — no! Why, if
I dropped in the effort to raise those who are
slighted, ignored, misunderstood, the effort to put
upon a conspicuous pillar intellects whose light
would illumine the whole world, if I dropped in
my struggle to do this, it would be a sacrifice —
not a waste!

DUDLEY.

A woman's only battles should be those of her
husband, the intellects she should develop are
those of her children. Ah, all you find in this
new life is mere buzz and noise — forgetfulness of
the wretched years of your mistaken marriage.

LADY VIVASH.

Mr. Silchester!

DUDLEY.

If the task you have undertaken is so fit and so
noble, why isn't your daughter Sylvia by your side
to share it?

LADY VIVASH.

Sylvia! my dear little Sylvia!

DUDLEY.

Why isn't she under your wing?

LADY VIVASH.

I think a young girl needs a different atmos-
phere. I mean, Lady Gillingham was going to
Italy, and offered to — I thought it best that Lady
Gillingham should — Oh, Sylvia has no troubles to
forget!

DUDLEY.

I am right, then!

LADY VIVASH.

And if you *are* — if what I am searching for is
but a sort of intoxication, an oblivion — how could
you, with your reminder of the past, help me?

DUDLEY.

By devoting myself to you — by loving away
the memory of your misfortunes.

LADY VIVASH.

[*After hiding her face for a moment.*] Dudley!
[*He stands by her side; she looks up to him and
takes his hand.*] Thank you, dear old friend.
But — it is so impossible.

DUDLEY.

Don't you love me at all?

LADY VIVASH.

Yes, I do love you; but don't you guess that I
can't forget —

DUDLEY.

Philip Lyster!

LADY VIVASH.

Philip Lyster. Ah, Dudley, — brother, if you
will be that, — it is years ago, but I loved Philip
so well! Eighteen years ago, and, oh, the fresh-
ness of it all to-day!

DUDLEY.

You parted not friends.

LADY VIVASH.

A boy-and-girl quarrel, with the girl in the
wrong. He was tender, chivalrous, sensitive; I,
wilful, capricious, cruel!

DUDLEY.

He left England?

LADY VIVASH.

I heard so. And then came my sin. Heaven
forgive me! Marrying another to spite the man
my temper had driven away from me.

DUDLEY.

You suffered!

LADY VIVASH.

I deserved it. Child as I was, I deserved it.
But he, so beyond me; why should I have ruined
his life? There, Dudley, is the misery that de-
stroys my peace. The news of my marriage must
have reached him in some foreign country. I can
see it coming to him, without a word of warning,
through some newspaper. I can hear his bitter
cry of contempt for the girl he had loved. Sometimes I think he must be dead, and I picture him
dying, lonely, uncared for. And sometimes I think
he lives on, old, broken, a misanthrope, the name
of woman the only jest to draw a smile from him.

[*She turns away crying.*

DUDLEY.

Ah — so that's your answer, Mary. My old friend Philip still stands between you and me.

LADY VIVASH.

Still — always —

Enter PETCH *with a telegram.*

PETCH.

A telegram, please.

[DUDLEY *takes it from the salver.*

DUDLEY.

I beg your pardon — Lady Vivash.

[*Giving the telegram to* LADY VIVASH. PETCH *goes out.* LADY VIVASH *reads the telegram.*]

LADY VIVASH.

Oh!

DUDLEY.

Nothing wrong, I hope?

LADY VIVASH.

Wrong? No! [*Brushing the tears from her eyes.*] Listen! Listen! It is from Victoria — you know — Lady Gillingham! It says [*reading*], "Our letters written to you at San Remo just discovered at the bottom of a trunk — never posted — we are home — shall come on to you!" Dudley, my Syl-

via, my little girl, is in London, and I didn't know!
[*Excitedly.*] Advise me. What shall I do? Shall
I go to Lady Gillingham's? I may miss them —
they may not be there. I want to see Sylvia so
badly! [*Stamping her foot.*] Dudley, you don't
tell me what to do.

DUDLEY.

[*Shaking his head.*] O you strong-minded
woman!

LADY VIVASH.

I'm not! I mean, I haven't seen her for so long.

DUDLEY.

They're sure to be here almost directly.

LADY VIVASH.

What am I to do till almost directly?

DUDLEY.

There's the committee down-stairs.

LADY VIVASH.

[*Impatiently.*] Oh!

DUDLEY.

And your speech to prepare for to-night.

LADY VIVASH.

I can't think of anything now but Sylvia!

DUDLEY.

No; and it is from this material that we are to
mould our cabinet ministers of the future!

The door opens, and MRS. BOYLE-CHEWTON,
MR. BARGUS *and* RHODA *enter.*

MRS. BOYLE-CHEWTON.

My dear Mary, you are forgetting the business
of to-day entirely.

LADY VIVASH.

I've had a telegram from Lady Gillingham.

MRS. BOYLE-CHEWTON.

Indeed!   The committee think it advisable —

LADY VIVASH.

Lady Gillingham and Sylvia are in London!

MRS. BOYLE-CHEWTON.

Very sudden.   The committee think that you
and Mr. Bargus —

LADY VIVASH.

They have been found at the bottom of a trunk.

MRS. BOYLE-CHEWTON.

Lady Gillingham and Sylvia!

LADY VIVASH.

No, no!

Mrs. Boyle-Chewton.

Then *who* has been found at the bottom of a trunk?

Lady Vivash.

Their letters — advising me of their return home.

Mrs. Boyle-Chewton.

How careless! The committee —

Lady Vivash.

Never posted — fancy!

Mrs. Boyle-Chewton.

My dear Mary!

Lady Vivash.

[*Handing* Mrs. Boyle-Chewton *the telegram.*] There it is.

Mrs. Boyle-Chewton.

[*Taking the telegram without reading it.*] Thank you. The committee have expressed an opinion —

Lady Vivash.

Oh, do read the telegram! [Mrs. Boyle-Chewton *reads the telegram. To* Rhoda.] You'll be friends with my Sylvia, won't you? Her pet name is Gossamer — she is so light and bright and merry.

Rhoda.

[*Thoughtfully.*] Bright and merry!

Mrs. Boyle-Chewton.

I never heard of such negligence. [*Returning
the telegram.*] Women like Lady Gillingham are
our stumbling-blocks.   Oh, for more concrete
minds!   Mr. Bargus, will *you* explain to Lady
Vivash?

Bargus.

The committee suggest that we compare the
salient features of our speeches, Lady Vivash, to
avoid a collision of ideas.   I shall be delighted —

Lady Vivash.

[*Absently, as she re-reads the telegram.*]   Quite
so — yes — certainly.

Bargus.

Shall I rapidly float over the surface of my in-
tentions, or will you?

Lady Vivash.

You — you first, please.

Bargus.

Thank you.   [*Producing a roll of paper.*]   The
question is in a nutshell.   The position of woman
is a social anomaly.

Lady Vivash.

Two women wouldn't travel all night from Paris
to London, would they?   Oh, I beg your pardon!

BARGUS.

Quite so. I ask — of what is woman capable ?

LADY VIVASH.

[*Pondering.*] Sleeping at Dover — rising early
— and catching the first train to town — that's
what they've done !

BARGUS.

Pardon me, Lady Vivash, I don't see —

LADY VIVASH.

No — of course — I haven't shown it to you,
have I ? [*Handing him the telegram.*] Lady Gillingham's telegram.

BARGUS.

But this doesn't say anything about the meeting !

LADY VIVASH.

You don't read it — we shall meet here.

BARGUS.

But the Union of Independent Women ?

LADY VIVASH.

Oh, don't bother about that !

Enter PETCH.

PETCH.

Lady Gillingham and Miss Vivash !

LADY VIVASH.

Sylvia! Sylvia!

[BARGUS *retires in astonishment.* SYLVIA, *a pretty, simple, fair-haired girl, about seventeen, dressed very lightly and tastefully, runs on, and is clasped in* LADY VIVASH'S *arms ;* LADY GILLINGHAM, *a handsomely dressed woman of thirty-three or thereabouts, with an elegant carriage and pleasing manner, following.* PETCH *goes out.*]

LADY VIVASH.

My dear little gossamer! Oh! how prètty you look! My sweet! [*Kissing* LADY GILLINGHAM.] Victoria, dear, how are you? What a surprise you give me! Lady Gillingham, Sylvia — you have met Mrs. Boyle-Chewton, haven't you? You both know Mr. Silchester. Rhoda, this is Sylvia.

[*The two girls look at each other with curiosity.*

SYLVIA.

[*Putting out her hand shyly.*] How do you do?

[RHODA *takes her hand, and then turns to* DUDLEY.

RHODA.

[*To* DUDLEY.] What luck some girls have, Uncle Dud!

SYLVIA.

[*To* LADY VIVASH.] Mamma, how strange you all look!

Mrs. Boyle-Chewton.

[*With a heave of resignation.*] I think *I* had better hear Mr. Bargus's plans for to-night. I fancy some of us are not sufficiently sympathetic towards Mr. Bargus. [*To* Bargus.] Will you walk into the garden? That will enable Lady Vivash to chat over lighter matters with Lady Gillingham.

[Mrs. Boyle-Chewton *and* Bargus *go out through the window, and are seen at intervals walking up and down and conversing earnestly.*]

Lady Gillingham.

[*Quietly to* Lady Vivash.] Send Sylvia away; I want to speak to you.

Lady Vivash.

Is anything wrong?

Lady Gillingham.

I hope you won't think so.

Lady Vivash.

Rhoda, will you show Sylvia the garden?
[Rhoda *and* Sylvia *go towards the window.*

Sylvia.

[*Catching sight of the printed bill.*] Oh, what's that? Is mamma going to sing at a concert?

LADY VIVASH.

[*Stamping her foot.*] Oh!

DUDLEY.

[*To* LADY VIVASH.] I'll explain — nicely.
[*He follows* RHODA *and* SYLVIA *out into the
garden.*]

LADY GILLINGHAM.

My dear Mary, I am afraid you will be very
angry with me.

LADY VIVASH.

What has happened ?

LADY GILLINGHAM.

Something very dreadful, or very pleasant —
just as you take it.

LADY VIVASH.

O Victoria!

LADY GILLINGHAM.

You intrusted dear little Gossamer to my
charge, and I need not tell you that I have tried
to do my duty.

LADY VIVASH.

Yes, yes, yes!

LADY GILLINGHAM.

You know, dear, they say Love laughs at lock-
smiths; that he may do, but he certainly ignores
chaperons.

LADY VIVASH.

Love! What do you mean?

LADY GILLINGHAM.

I knew you would be angry; but it is not my fault. Gossamer is in love, dear — there!

LADY VIVASH.

Gossamer in love! Gossamer in love! And of course somebody is in love with her?

LADY GILLINGHAM.

Oh, yes, dear, of course — that happened first.

LADY VIVASH.

Who — who is it?

LADY GILLINGHAM.

There, Mary, you've upset me with your first question. Who is it? I suppose from an old-fashioned point of view I ought to say, Nobody. But Lord Gillingham says that nowadays everybody with a coat and waistcoat is somebody, especially if he be an American, and this gentleman is an American.

LADY VIVASH.

An American?

LADY GILLINGHAM.

Yes; from Vermont. But he doesn't of course whittle a stick or do those amusing things we read about. Have you ever heard of Ira Lee, the American poet?

LADY VIVASH.

I don't know — I dare say — I can't remember.

LADY GILLINGHAM.

Get him from Mudie's, Mary, at once. Gossamer's lover is Ira Lee. We met him in Florence, at Mrs. Rocksavage's. Of course he was smitten with Sylvia; every one has been, from a Charing-Cross porter to the Pope. ·

LADY VIVASH.

But she — she?

LADY GILLINGHAM.

She was only interested at first, till she read his poetry, and then — well, get him from Mudie's. I heard a portion of his history — quite romantic. Some time ago he banished himself out West into the Colorado Mountains, leading a sort of camp-life with some horribly rough, outcast people — fancy, Mary! A thing I couldn't do! Then he wrote plaintive verses about the wrongs of the Indians, and their loves, until an enterprising person came along and bought his poetry, or borrowed it, — I forget which, — and published it in New York. And there they christened him the Poet of the Prairies. And now he's rich, and I suppose has had enough of the Indians, who are a very untidy race, and he is seeing Europe. There, Mary; what do you think of it all?

[BARGUS *is seen rehearsing his speech to* MRS. BOYLE-CHEWTON *outside the window.*]

LADY VIVASH.

Tell me — tell me what you have done!

LADY GILLINGHAM.

Well, dear, I have done what I consider the very wisest thing — I have done nothing. Mr. Lee gave me to understand that he admired Sylvia — she gave me to understand that she loved Mr. Lee. I said "Very well, then, we'll go home."

LADY VIVASH.

And he?

LADY GILLINGHAM.

He said, "Do — and I'll follow you."

LADY VIVASH.

Oh, what shall I do?

LADY GILLINGHAM.

See him, dear.

LADY VIVASH.

See him!

LADY GILLINGHAM.

He's most anxious to do everything *in formâ* — what is it? Not *pauperis — proprietas; in formâ proprietas.* See him, and accept him or reject him.

[SYLVIA, RHODA, *and* DUDLEY *appear outside the window.*]

LADY VIVASH.

Reject *him* — yes. But Sylvia?

LADY GILLINGHAM.

Why, at the worst, it is only a child's first love
— nothing more.

LADY VIVASH.

It need be nothing more.   Ah, I know what the
child's first love means to the grown woman!

SYLVIA *re-enters the room.*

SYLVIA.

Mamma, won't you — [*She stops suddenly,
looking into* LADY VIVASH's *face.*] Lady Gillingham has been speaking to you about me!

LADY VIVASH.

Yes, dear.

SYLVIA.

I — I am so sorry, mamma.

LADY VIVASH.

Sorry?

SYLVIA.

So sorry that — that Mr. Lee cannot get to London until Wednesday.

[LADY GILLINGHAM *goes to* RHODA *and*
DUDLEY, *outside in the garden.*]

LADY VIVASH.

[*Drawing* SYLVIA *to her and stroking her head.*]
Do you really love him, Gossamer ?

SYLVIA.

I think I do — really.

LADY VIVASH.

And if I told you that it is impossible, absurd —
that a child's first foolish fancy is to be checked,
laughed at, and forgotten — what then ?

SYLVIA.

Then I should know you were not in earnest.

LADY VIVASH.

Not in earnest ?

SYLVIA.

No. Mamma, do you remember, once when you
were in bitter trouble, taking me upon your lap and
telling me of *your* first love ?

LADY VIVASH.

Gossamer — yes !

SYLVIA.

Of some one who came to Bruges, painting, just
before you left your school — some friend of Mr.
Silchester's ?

LADY VIVASH.

Yes.

SYLVIA.

He followed you to London — you loved him, mamma dear; you told me so!

LADY VIVASH.

[*In a whisper, trembling.*] Ah, yes!

SYLVIA.

But one day in a fit of jealousy you sent him away from you, and you never saw him again.

LADY VIVASH.

Never again!

SYLVIA.

But "Sylvia," you said to me, "a woman's first love is her religion; if its object be worthy it will sanctify her whole life." And, mamma, that is why I know you will let me go on loving Mr. Lee.

LADY VIVASH.

[*With a cry of tenderness, pressing* SYLVIA *to her.*] My darling! my darling!

PETCH *enters with a small bundle of letters upon a salver.*

PETCH.

Lady Gillingham's carriage!

LADY GILLINGHAM.

[*Re-entering the room.*] Oh, how time flies! Mary, I must catch the two o'clock train to Ketterby. I have promised to fetch Lord Gillingham up to town.

PETCH.

[*Giving letters to* DUDLEY, *who has come into the room.*] Your servant has just brought these letters, sir, in case you might not return home till late.

DUDLEY.

Thank you.

[PETCH *goes out as* BARGUS *comes in, followed by* MRS BOYLE-CHEWTON.]

LADY GILLINGHAM.

[*To* LADY VIVASH.] Do let me take Sylvia with me to Ketterby!

LADY VIVASH.

Oh, no, no! We have been so long parted.

LADY GILLINGHAM.

My dear Mary, we shall return to town on Wednesday — the day after to-morrow.

MRS. BOYLE-CHEWTON.

In *my* opinion, on the eve of our great meeting even the society of her daughter is a most dangerous distraction to Lady Vivash.

LADY GILLINGHAM.

I think so too, and I've a delicious plan in my head. On Wednesday night Lord Gillingham and I have some friends and some music at Kensington

— all sorts of dear, nice people : you will come, of course, Mary ?

MRS. BOYLE-CHEWTON.

Um — on Wednesday night *we* have a Financial Committee.

LADY GILLINGHAM.

And if dear Mrs. Boyle-Chewton will dispense with ceremony and bring her daughter —

MRS. BOYLE-CHEWTON.

H'm ! I shall be glad to carry my opinions and convictions into alien circles.   Thank you, Lady Gillingham.

LADY GILLINGHAM.

[*To* DUDLEY.]   Mr. Silchester, I depend on you too, and —

MRS. BOYLE-CHEWTON.

[*Introducing* MR. BARGUS.]   Lady Gillingham — my friend and associate, Mr. Clarence Bargus, Member for the Skipping-Molton Division of Cuddleford.

LADY GILLINGHAM.

And perhaps Mr. Bargus —

MRS. BOYLE-CHEWTON.

Mr. Bargus will be very happy.

BARGUS.

[*Nervously.*]   Very happy — delighted !   [*To himself, with an eye on* LADY GILLINGHAM.]   Exceedingly pretty woman. [*Checking himself.*] Ahem! tush!

LADY GILLINGHAM.

I'll send cards to you all to-night. [*Quietly to* LADY VIVASH.] Mary, Mr. Ira Lee will be there; he reaches London on Wednesday morning. Don't you see my scheme? You will be able to survey him before he makes his first advances.

PETCH *re-enters.*

PETCH.

Lady Gillingham's coachman says he can only just get to the station in time.

LADY GILLINGHAM.

Oh, dear! my husband hasn't seen me for four months — he'll think it so odd if I miss the train. [*Kissing* LADY VIVASH.] Good-by, Mary. I may have Sylvia, may I not? [LADY VIVASH *embraces* SYLVIA *passionately.*] Good-by, every-body — till Wednesday. Good-by! Good-by! Good-by! Sylvia!

[*Going to the door,* SYLVIA *running after her.*

LADY VIVASH.

Sylvia! [SYLVIA *returns to* LADY VIVASH, *who embraces her again.*] Gossamer, you won't forget me — your mother — will you?

SYLVIA.

O mamma dear!

LADY GILLINGHAM.

[*Impatiently.*] Oh, dear! Oh, dear!

SYLVIA.

[*Going.*] Good-by! Good-by! Good-by!

[LADY GILLINGHAM *and* SYLVIA *go out,
followed by* PETCH.

MRS. BOYLE-CHEWTON.

And now, if Lady Vivash's mind is quite clear,
Mr. Bargus will resume.

BARGUS.

[*Oratorically.*] The question is in a nutshell.
Of what is woman capable? Woman is —

DUDLEY.

[*Who has been opening and reading his letters.*]
Good heavens! [*To* BARGUS.] I beg your pardon — allow me, one moment!

MRS. BOYLE-CHEWTON.

Really, Dudley!

DUDLEY.

[*Softly, to* LADY VIVASH, *who has dropped thoughtfully into a chair.*] Lady Vivash — Mary! I'm a
poor unlucky devil, but I'm not so wrapped up in
myself that I can't feel glad at bringing you this
good news.

LADY VIVASH.

Good news!

DUDLEY.

Strange news!   Philip Lyster is living.

LADY VIVASH.

Living!

DUDLEY.

And in England — or will be almost directly.
[*Handing her a letter.*]   Look!

LADY VIVASH.

[*With a gasp.*]   Philip's — writing!

DUDLEY.

Read it.

LADY VIVASH.

[*Trying to read the letter.*]   I can't — I can't —
make it out.   Tell me what he says.

[*She returns the letter.   DUDLEY stands by
her side ; she sits staring forward eagerly.*

DUDLEY.

It is written from Paris, yesterday.   [*Reading.*]
"My dear Dudley.   The dead returned to life!   I
have come into your world again — changed — another man — but still your friend as of old, if you
will have it so.   I don't quite know the hour of
my reaching England, but I do know that I am to
burst upon London society next Wednesday night
at a party at Lord Gillingham's " —

LADY VIVASH.

Oh!

DUDLEY.

[*Resuming.*] " Come to me at Stark's Hotel at latest the day following. — PHILIP LYSTER."

LADY VIVASH.

At Lord Gillingham's?

DUDLEY.

Lady Gillingham didn't mention —

LADY VIVASH.

She doesn't know that Philip and I were ever acquainted. Philip! Come back!

DUDLEY.

Come back — yes. I think, Mary, I *shall* go to Palermo after all. [*To* BARGUS.] I beg your pardon.

MRS. BOYLE-CHEWTON.

Now, Mr. Bargus.

BARGUS.

The question is in a nutshell. Of what is woman capable?

MRS. BOYLE-CHEWTON.

Mary, pray listen!

BARGUS.

Is this superficial sentiment, which is so popular, called love, to be the only —

LADY VIVASH.

Come back! come back!

MRS. BOYLE-CHEWTON.

Mary!

LADY VIVASH.

I — I can't remain. I — I am going out!

MRS. BOYLE-CHEWTON.

Going out!

LADY VIVASH.

To Madame Lisette's.

MRS. BOYLE-CHEWTON.

To Madame Lisette. Not the dressmaker!

LADY VIVASH.

Yes. I — I must look something like my old self on Wednesday night!

    [She rushes out. They look after her in consternation.]

END OF THE FIRST ACT.

THE SECOND ACT

The scene is a richly appointed ante-room at LORD
GILLINGHAM'S, *with a large opening leading
to the drawing-rooms, and showing a distant
conservatory with a fountain playing. On the
right is a recess furnished with settees, palms,
and candelabra, over the entrance to which is a
curtain fastened back. On the left are large
French windows opening into the garden, which
is bright with moonlight.*

There is the sound of music in the distance. MR.
WADE GREEN *is sitting in the corner with his
eyes closed. He is a young man, with weak
eyes, spectacles, and little perky whiskers.
When nobody is looking at him his countenance
is most melancholy, but directly he is observed
he assumes a facetious expression.* LADY LIP-
TROTT, *a tall, gaunt, withered woman, with a
deep, gruff voice and black ringlets, dressed
showily, but in execrable taste, and the* HON.
GEORGE LIPTROTT, *her son, an insipid, ultra-
modern young gentleman, stroll in from the
garden.*

62

LADY LIPTROTT.

George.

GEORGE.

Yes, ma?

LADY LIPTROTT.

We'll sit about in the music-room for half an hour, and then go on to the Beauchamps'. The Gillinghams' entertainments are always so insufferably tiresome.

GEORGE.

Yes, it's awfully slow, ma. [GREEN, *hearing voices, rises, yawns wearily, shakes himself, and emerges from the corner with his most humorous expression.*] H'are yah?

GREEN.

H'are yah? [GREEN *loiters away.*

LADY LIPTROTT.

[*To* GEORGE.] I know that man's face — who is he?

GEORGE.

Why, ma, that's Wade Green, the man who's so awfully entertaining at the piano with those frightfully amusing songs — don't you know? When he sings it's as much as people can do to keep from laughing. [*To* GREEN.] H'are yah?

GREEN.

[*Stifling a yawn and turning briskly.*] You quite well?

GEORGE.

Thanks.   You going to sing?

GREEN.

Um.   A little thing of last season's.

GEORGE.

Haw?   Then do you go on to the Beauchamps'
by any chance?

GREEN.

I shall pop in.

GEORGE.

Will you sing thah?

GREEN.

Ye-es.   A little thing I used to do years ago.

GEORGE.

Haw!   Were you at Mrs. Phillamore's this
afternoon?

GREEN.

Yes.   Very enjoyable.

GEORGE.

Did you sing thah?

GREEN.

Oh, a little thing they always ask for; one of
my old little things.

GEORGE.

Haw! It will be awful fun when you do something new, won't it?

[*As* GREEN *walks away he meets* LORD
GILLINGHAM *entering, a handsome old
gentleman, slightly deaf.*]

LORD GILLINGHAM.

Ah, Mr. Green, they miss you very much in there.

GREEN.

[*Raising his voice.*] Just going in — just going in.

[*He still loiters about with his hands in his
pockets.*]

LORD GILLINGHAM.

[*Seeing* LADY LIPTROTT.] You're not going, are you? Lady Gillingham has been looking for you. There's some music in there.

LADY LIPTROTT.

[*Raising her voice.*] What a charming night!

LORD GILLINGHAM.

Outside?

LADY LIPTROTT.

Here.

LORD GILLINGHAM.

[*Courteously.*] So glad.

LADY LIPTROTT.

[*To* GEORGE.] That man is breaking up.

GEORGE.

Rapidly.

LORD GILLINGHAM.

Ah, George!

GEORGE.

[*Raising his voice.*] Delighted you're looking
so much bettah.

[LORD GILLINGHAM *smiles and nods, but as*
LADY LIPTROTT *and* GEORGE *go out he
gapes wearily;* GREEN, *who is saunter-
ing about aimlessly, does the same; they
turn, and surprise each other at it.*]

GREEN.

[*Rather embarrassed, resuming his comic manner.*
Hah! um! Yes — I'm — I'm just going in — just
going in.   [*He disappears quickly.*

A servant enters.

SERVANT.

[*Announcing.*] Mr. and Mrs. Hawley Hill.

MR. *and* MRS. HAWLEY HILL, *a stout couple, enter,
but* LORD GILLINGHAM *has his back to them,
and does not notice them.*

HAWLEY HILL.

We can't give them long, Adelaide.

MRS. HAWLEY HILL.

Isn't that Lord Gillingham?   [*They approach.*

LORD GILLINGHAM.

[*Smiling pleasantly.*] You are not going, are
you? Lady Gillingham has been looking for you.
There's some music in there.

MRS. HAWLEY HILL.

[*Raising her voice.*] Just come.

LORD GILLINGHAM.

Eh?

MRS. HAWLEY HILL.

We've just come.

LORD GILLINGHAM.

Oh, how d'ye do? How d'ye do? Let us find
my wife.

[*He takes them towards the drawing-rooms.*

SERVANT.

[*Announcing.*] Mr. Silchester.

Enter DUDLEY SILCHESTER.

LORD GILLINGHAM.

[*To the* HILLS.] Ah, there she is!

MR. AND MRS. HAWLEY HILL.

My dear Lady Gillingham —   [*They go out.*

LORD GILLINGHAM.

[*Seeing* DUDLEY.] You're not going, are you?
Lady Gillingham has been looking for you; there's
some music in there.

DUDLEY.

Just come! How are you?

LORD GILLINGHAM.

Ah! How are you? Mr. Silchester, isn't it?

DUDLEY.

How's Lady Gillingham?

LORD GILLINGHAM.

Very well. She's better than I am at a party
— I get dazed. Lady Gillingham is a wonderful
woman. I was born too long ago for her. That's
my great fault.

DUDLEY.

[*Sympathetically.*] Ah!

LORD GILLINGHAM.

Yes. [*They stand side by side on the hearth-rug.*

DUDLEY.

Fine May!

LORD GILLINGHAM.

Very. Very fine May.

DUDLEY.

One of the finest Mays I remember.

LORD GILLINGHAM.
English Mays.

DUDLEY.
I mean English Mays.

LORD GILLINGHAM.
May is a fine month abroad.

DUDLEY.
Yes — sometimes.

LORD GILLINGHAM.
Ah, I mean sometimes.

[*They turn their heads from each other and gape.*

DUDLEY.
Is Lyster here?

LORD GILLINGHAM.
What Lyster is that?

DUDLEY.
Philip Lyster — Gerald Lyster's son. Went away suddenly years and years ago.

LORD GILLINGHAM.
Don't know him.

DUDLEY.
He wrote to tell me he'd be here to-night.

Lord Gillingham.

Oh, very likely, very likely! There are a great many people here I don't know. A friend of my wife's, perhaps. Come along.

[Lady Gillingham, *richly dressed, enters.*

Lady Gillingham.

[*Shaking hands with* Dudley.] How do you do? So pleased! [*Surprising* Lord Gilling- ham *in the middle of a gape.*] Theodore! people are looking for you. You're horrid. [*To* Dud- ley.] He leaves everything to me.

Dudley.

I wish he'd leave something to me. I mean I wish I might assist you. [*To himself.*] Con- found it! what a stupid thing to say!

[Sylvia *enters with the* Hon. George Lip- trott. *She is dressed simply but charm- ingly in white; she greets* Dudley, *then strolls with* George *to the recess.*]

George.

Haw! do you ever go to Lord's?

Sylvia.

Lord's Cricket Ground? Oh, yes.

George.

Eton and Harrow?

Sylvia.

Yes.

GEORGE.

Were you thah the yeah before last?

SYLVIA.

Yes; I was.

GEORGE.

Really?

SYLVIA.

Really.

GEORGE.

Then you saw me thah! I played for Eton the yeah before last.

SYLVIA.

Oh!

GEORGE.

Isn't the world absurdly small? The ideah of your being thah when I was thah! Both thah!

[*They sit talking.*

SERVANT.

[*Announcing.*] Mrs. Boyle-Chewton, Miss Boyle-Chewton, and Mr. Bargus.

DUDLEY.

Oh, lor! the political infant! [*Goes out quickly.*

LADY GILLINGHAM.

[*In* LORD GILLINGHAM'S *ear.*] Here are those people — Mary's friends — the strong-minded ladies — and Mr. Bargus.

MRS. BOYLE-CHEWTON, RHODA, *and* MR. BARGUS
*enter, the ladies dressed very plainly in
sombre silks.*

LADY GILLINGHAM.

How do you do? How do you do? So delighted! [*Introducing.*] Lord Gillingham! [*To* MRS. BOYLE-CHEWTON.] Is Mary with you?

MRS. BOYLE-CHEWTON.

[*Grimly.*] No. I left Lady Vivash deeply engaged with Madame Lisette, the dressmaker.

LORD GILLINGHAM.

[*To* BARGUS.] Certainly; very interesting — very interesting.

BARGUS.

My lord, it is a great question in a nutshell! The position of Woman —

LORD GILLINGHAM.

Quite so; yesterday's paper reported your speech very fully.

[LADY LIPTROTT *re-enters, and is introduced to* MRS. BOYLE-CHEWTON.]

LADY GILLINGHAM.

[*To* RHODA.] There is Sylvia.

[RHODA *goes to* SYLVIA, *who rises to meet her.*

SYLVIA.

Oh, I'm so glad! Has mamma come?

RHODA.

No.

SYLVIA.

How late she is!   Do sit by me for a moment.

[*They sit side by side.   Rising,* GEORGE
finds RHODA *next to him instead of*
SYLVIA.]

GEORGE.

Haw!   I think I'll just — if you don't mind —
I'll look for my mother!   [*To himself.*]   What a
dowdy girl!

LADY LIPTROTT.

[*To* GEORGE, *as they meet.*]   George, look at
that extraordinarily dressed person!

GEORGE.

Yes.   I've just seen anothah!

LADY LIPTROTT.

Ugh! how women can so disfigure themselves I
can't imagine.   Let us retain the soft docility and
gentle exterior which are Heaven's gifts, or let us
die.   Give me some air outside.

[*They go into the garden.*

LADY GILLINGHAM.

We mustn't miss Bandinelli, the new violinist.

[BARGUS *bobs and bows nervously;* LORD
GILLINGHAM *gallantly escorts* MRS.
BOYLE-CHEWTON.]

MRS. BOYLE-CHEWTON.

[*To* LORD GILLINGHAM.]   Why don't you become one of us?

LORD GILLINGHAM.

Madam, I am all yours.

MRS. BOYLE-CHEWTON.

Join our Union.

LORD GILLINGHAM.

Ah, I haven't thought about it.

MRS. BOYLE-CHEWTON.

Why can't women vote ?

LORD GILLINGHAM.

They can — they tell the men how to.

MRS. BOYLE-CHEWTON.

Why can't women sit ?

LORD GILLINGHAM.

[*Puzzled.*] They can — can't they ?

MRS. BOYLE-CHEWTON.

I mean in the House of Commons ! Rhoda !

RHODA.

Yes, mamma. [BARGUS *and* LADY GILLING-HAM, LORD GILLINGHAM, *and* MRS. BOYLE-CHEW-TON *go into the drawing-rooms.* RHODA *rises.*] I suppose I must go, but I hate it.

SYLVIA.

Hate it !

RHODA.

I'm not dressed very nicely; people stare so.

SYLVIA.

[*Putting her arm around her waist.*] Shall I come with you?

[RHODA *disengages herself, looking at* SYL-VIA'S *dress and then at her own.*

RHODA.

Oh, no; please don't! Besides, you will want to get rid of me directly Mr. Lee arrives.

SYLVIA.

Mr. Lee! O Rhoda, dear, who told you?

RHODA.

Nobody. I heard Lady Vivash telling mamma.

SYLVIA.

[*Taking* RHODA'S *hand.*] Oh, I'm glad you know; for I do want to talk about him so much. He's dark, you know, and is a poet; they call him the "Poet of the Prairies," in his own country. He's an American, with a soft, low voice. We've only seen each other three times and a little bit. We met in Florence. Do you think it's romantic? You can buy his poems at the railway station. They're a shilling. Look! [*Taking from her pocket a little volume bound in red silk.*] There they are. I put them in that bright cover. I *did* say he was dark, didn't I? Oh, aren't I telling you all about him?

RHODA.

[*Superciliously.*]   You are, rather.

SYLVIA.

You're not cross, are you?   I do hope you'll be
engaged soon.

RHODA.

[*Biting her lips.*]   Do you?   Thank you.   Perhaps I'm as much engaged as you appear to be.

SYLVIA.

Oh, I'm so glad!   Tell me who it is — oh, do!

RHODA.

If I choose, it is Mr. Bargus.

SYLVIA.

[*Horrified.*]   Mr. Bargus!   Oh, don't!

RHODA.

[*In a rage.*]   I don't know why you should
make that face.   Mr. Bargus is a member of Parliament.   A member of Parliament ranks higher
than a poet.

SYLVIA.

Oh, I don't think that's a nice thing to say; and
Lady Gillingham has told me that there are members *and* members.   Besides, a man isn't born a
member of Parliament.   Mr. Lee was born a poet.

RHODA.

Indeed! He'd better go back, then; they're doing away with hereditary privileges in this country.

SERVANT.

[*Announcing.*] Mr. Lee!

SYLVIA.

Oh!

IRA LEE *enters. He is a tall, handsome man of about thirty-seven, with a gentle, self-contained manner.*

LEE.

[*Advancing to* SYLVIA *with a pleasant smile.*] Miss Vivash.

SYLVIA.

[*Hanging her head.*] Mr. Lee.

> [RHODA *stares at* LEE, *then turns to go as* BARGUS *enters.*]

BARGUS.

Miss Chewton — Rhoda. Your mamma has delegated me to fetch you.

> [RHODA *stares contemptuously at* LEE *and* SYLVIA, *and, seizing* BARGUS'S *arm, goes out with him.*]

LEE.

I didn't reach London until five o'clock this afternoon.

SYLVIA.

You must be very weary.

LEE.

Of being parted from you — ah, yes. Is Lady Vivash here ?

SYLVIA.

Not yet.

LEE.

Will she be very angry ?

SYLVIA.

I think she will be a little angry if you stay with me now.

LEE.

Very well, then ; I'll go and find Lady Gillingham. [*Taking her hand.*] Suppose your mother, for some reason, dislikes me exceedingly.

SYLVIA.

Oh, don't, please ! What is there not to like ?

LEE.

So much. Why, look at your little hand in mine ; it's like a rosebud on an old Delft plate. I have lived twice as long as you.

SYLVIA.

You are a poet ; you always will. Besides, I think mamma will like you for being rather old ; when she married my papa he was three times *her* age.

LEE.

No — was he ?

SYLVIA.

[*Surprised.*] Didn't you know ?

LEE.

Certainly not. You and I have never had time
to talk of anything but the future — and the
weather.

SYLVIA.

Oh, you're not curious, like women ! You could
have found out all about mamma — who she was,
whom she married, when she married, when I was
bor — everything. You ought to be curious about
me. I have read your poems.

LEE.

I don't want to know more than that you are
sweet and gentle, with a voice that has the meaning of truth in it.

SYLVIA.

But my mamma ?

LEE.

Oh, I have *imagined* her — a woman with eyes
like yours, only sadder ; lips like yours, only paler ;
a voice like yours, only deeper ; a woman whose
task in life it is to show her child how to grow old
beautifully !

SYLVIA.

Thank you. Now go and find Lady Gillingham.

[*He raises her hand to his lips tenderly.*

LEE.

Why shouldn't you show me the way to her?

SYLVIA.

It is such a little way.

LEE.

Isn't there a longer way to Lady Gillingham?

SYLVIA.

Oh, yes — through the garden; only it's *much* longer.

LEE.

Take me the much longer way. [*They walk a step or two towards the window; he stops and points to the book she still carries.*] May I carry that?

SYLVIA.

Oh! [*Handing him the book, which he opens.*] Do you think me very silly?

LEE.

I think you ought to be ordered a course of sounder reading.

SYLVIA.

Write your name there, please.

LEE.

[*Hesitating a moment.*] My name?

[*He takes a pencil from his pocket and writes his name; then shows it to her.*]

SYLVIA.

" Philip Lyster ! " Who's that ?

LEE.

Ira Lee.

SYLVIA.

Is Philip Lyster your real name ?

LEE.

It was real to me once.

SYLVIA.

I don't seem to know you now at all. [*Half-frightened.*] Philip — Lyster.

LEE.

Ira Lee or Philip Lyster — the man is the same.

[*Taking her hand and gently drawing it through his arm.*]

SYLVIA.

[*To herself.*] Philip Lyster.

[*They walk to the window ; the moon shines in upon them ; he turns to her.*]

LEE.

You trust me, Sylvia ?

SYLVIA.

Philip. [*Raising her eyes and looking into his face.*] Yes —

[*They disappear into the garden. As they go* LADY GILLINGHAM *enters quickly.*]

LADY GILLINGHAM.

Sylvia! Sylvia! Oh, where is Sylvia? As long as I live I'll never chaperon another unmarried girl. [*Looking into the corner.*] Oh, the dreadful responsibility! Sylvia!

SERVANT.

[*Announcing.*] Lady Vivash!

[LADY VIVASH *enters quickly. She is magnificently dressed ; her cheeks are bright, her eyes sparkling, her manner hurried and excited.*]

LADY GILLINGHAM.

Mary!

LADY VIVASH.

[*Kissing her upon the cheek.*] Victoria dear!

LADY GILLINGHAM.

Oh, how beautiful you look!

LADY VIVASH.

Beautiful ? Ah, I have never looked so ugly in my whole life.

LADY GILLINGHAM.

Nonsense! [*Laughing.*] What will Mrs. Boyle-
Chewton say? What a change!

LADY VIVASH.

Change! Yes.

LADY GILLINGHAM.

Since yesterday.

LADY VIVASH.

What a change since eighteen years ago!

LADY GILLINGHAM.

Mary, what is the matter? Come with me.

LADY VIVASH.

Is Sylvia well?

LADY GILLINGHAM.

[*Wonderingly.*] Yes; quite well.

LADY VIVASH.

Is her American — Mr. — Mr. Lee here?

LADY GILLINGHAM.

No; not yet, I think.

LADY VIVASH.

Lovers are not impatient nowadays. I — I —
am ready.

> [*Suddenly* LADY VIVASH *supports herself
> on* LADY GILLINGHAM'S *arm for a mo-
> ment, and then sits faintly.*]

LADY GILLINGHAM.

Mary, you are ill!

LADY VIVASH.

No; wait. I — I've something to say to you.
I didn't know — that — you — were acquainted
with — Mr. Lyster.

LADY GILLINGHAM.

Mr. Lyster?

LADY VIVASH.

Philip Lyster. I have never told you, but he
and I were — friends, years ago. Tell me — how
does he look? Stop; let me guess. Worn — with
silver hair at the temples — eyes that seem looking away, back. [*Pointing to the drawing-room.*]
Is he there? Shall I meet him? Don't notice
us. I shall know him! I shall know him! I
shall know him!

LADY GILLINGHAM.

Mary, *I* know no Mr. Lyster.

LADY VIVASH.

He is to be here — in your house — to-night! I
have seen his letter, his own handwriting!

LADY GILLINGHAM.

Then he must be somebody Theodore has invited without consulting me. Let us go and ask.

[*She goes to the drawing-room.*

LADY VIVASH.

Yes. [*Walking straight across to the mirror and looking into it earnestly.*] Then and now — then and now! Oh!

[*She turns with a low cry; then goes out as* BARGUS *enters with* MRS. BOYLE-CHEWTON *from the window, followed by* RHODA.]

BARGUS.

[*Nervously, apart to* RHODA.] Go away for five minutes.

RHODA.

[*Apart to him.*] What are you going to do?

BARGUS.

Break the news of our engagement to your dear mamma.

RHODA.

Not here!

BARGUS.

Certainly! Your dear mamma can't be violently angry here. [RHODA *goes out.*

MRS. BOYLE-CHEWTON.

You say you wish to speak to me, Mr. Bargus.

BARGUS.

H'm! Mrs. Boyle-Chewton, what I have on my — on my heart might have kept till to-morrow, or next week, but it weighs heavily, and I did not sleep last night for it; so it is better out. The

matter is in a nutshell, Mrs. Boyle-Chewton.   I
am a bachelor.

Mrs. Boyle-Chewton.

You are wedded to our cause, Mr. Bargus.

Bargus.

Politically ; politically, of course a man may be
wedded to many causes — some members are Mor-
mons. Politically I am all yours.

Mrs. Boyle-Chewton.

We appreciate you.

Bargus.

Thank you, I am sure you do; but, domestically,
I am all my own. Now, my dear lady, my senti-
ments concerning this very popular emotion, about
which we hear so much, called love, are known to
you. Love reminds me of the goose at one of our
little county dinners. There it is at the head of
the table, rich and tempting, all eyes upon it and
all mouths watering. Every plate is sent up, and
the carver, like Cupid, rises to the occasion — and
what is the result ? Only two out of a dozen get
a good cut, and before an hour is over those two
are extremely sorry for it. But, my dear lady,
marriage — two persons walking soberly through
life under one umbrella, cheerfully accepting the
drippings of Providence down the backs of their
necks — that's an elevating spectacle.

Mrs. Boyle-Chewton.

Really, Mr. Bargus, I don't see —

Bargus.

A moment — it is in a nutshell. Politically, I'm already a member of your charming establishment; politically, my slippers already nestle at your genial hearth. There's a great deal of trotting to and fro between Regent's Park and myself. Now, Mrs. Boyle-Chewton, — I put it humorously, — why shouldn't you spare me the journey *to* the Park in the morning, and *from* the Park in the afternoon?

Mrs. Boyle-Chewton.

Mr. Bargus!

Bargus.

Take a moment — take a moment!

Mrs. Boyle-Chewton.

It is so sudden. I have never suspected it. All my best friends will accuse me of husband-hunting.

Bargus.

They can't; they only say that when the lady concerned is not an extremely attractive creature.

Mrs. Boyle-Chewton.

[*Looking away.*] O Mr. Bargus!

Bargus.

They can't say that of a charming face and a most fascinating manner.

Mrs. Boyle-Chewton.

[*Turning to him warmly.*] Be quiet! I am disappointed in you. [*Simpering.*] You don't mean
it! [Lady Liptrott *and* George *enter from the
garden, and cross the room ;* Mrs. Boyle-Chewton
*immediately speaks loudly, with a change of man-
ner.*] The question of the amelioration of the condition of woman, Mr. Bargus, is one that may well
profit by the devotion of such great spirits as yourself, not to mention the modest labor— [Lady
Liptrott *and* George *go out by door ;* Mrs.
Boyle-Chewton *turns again to* Bargus.] I have
wandered from the point. Go on.

Bargus.

With regard to Rhoda, I fancy I am not obnox-
.ious to her.

Mrs. Boyle-Chewton.

Obnoxious, indeed !

Bargus.

The event will brighten her life.

Mrs. Boyle-Chewton.

I should think so !

Bargus.

Would you care to call me — Clarence ?

Mrs. Boyle-Chewton.

Not yet — not yet.

Bargus.

Not to oblige me?

Mrs. Boyle-Chewton.

No, no!

Bargus.

Not to delight me?

Mrs. Boyle-Chewton.

[*Impulsively.*] Clarence! [Mr. *and* Mrs. Hawley Hill *enter from the drawing-room, cross to the door. Loudly.*] What future may be in store for woman it is impossible to estimate or predict. But one great fact is assured — one great fact — [Mr. *and* Mrs. Hawley Hill *disappear.*] Clarence, will *you* speak to Rhoda?

Bargus.

Certainly; to-night. If Mr. Silchester is your escort, Rhoda and I might — ahem! — follow in a four-wheeler.

Mrs. Boyle-Chewton.

I don't think that's necessary!

Bargus.

No — perhaps not. Beg pardon.

Mrs. Boyle-Chewton.

And I have still one condition to impose upon you.

BARGUS.

A hundred — a hundred.

MRS. BOYLE-CHEWTON.

[*Pointing to the recess.*] Sha'n't we be less liable to interruption in there?

BARGUS.

Shall we? [*To himself.*] I wish she'd let me get away to Rhoda!   [*They sit side by side.*

MRS. BOYLE-CHEWTON.

Clarence, you will not avail yourself of our new relationship to distract my thoughts from the mighty work of woman's emancipation?

BARGUS.

[*Edging away nervously.*] My dear Mrs. Boyle-Chewton, certainly not — certainly not. Why should I?

MRS. BOYLE-CHEWTON.

You will not allow your affection for the wife to weaken your co-operation with the agitator?

BARGUS.

[*Aghast, his eyes staring from his head.*] Not allow my affec — my aff — ! I beg your pardon!

MRS. BOYLE-CHEWTON.

You know what I hint at. You won't take me away for our honeymoon till Parliament has risen?

BARGUS.

[*Wildly.*] Mrs. Boyle-Chewton!

[DUDLEY *and* RHODA *come from the drawing-room together.*]

MRS. BOYLE-CHEWTON.

Hush! don't kneel! [*Rising and looking around
the corner.*] Dudley!

DUDLEY.

Oh, are you there, Edith?

MRS. BOYLE-CHEWTON.

[*In a childish voice.*] Yes!

[*She approaches them, trying to conceal*
BARGUS, *who sinks back.*]

BARGUS.

[*To himself, with horror.*] I see it! It's all in
a nutshell. The mother has taken it to herself.
Oh, I've gone into the wrong lobby!

MRS. BOYLE-CHEWTON.

[*Pointing to the recess.*] I think Mr. Bargus is
there.

DUDLEY.

Is he? [*To himself.*] Oh, yes; there's the infant. [BARGUS *advances falteringly.*] How d'ye
do? [BARGUS *nods, but cannot speak.*

Mrs. Boyle-Chewton.

Dudley dear — Rhoda — we three are of one family. I — I think Mr. Bargus has something to tell you.

Dudley.

Indeed !

Mrs. Boyle-Chewton.

Something I hope most interesting to Rhoda — my child.

Rhoda.

O mamma !

Mrs. Boyle-Chewton.

Already united to us by ties of sympathy, Mr. Bargus asks that he may be allowed to add one more link to the chain by becoming — Rhoda's father.

Rhoda.

[*Clenching her hands.*] Oh !

Dudley.

Good gracious !

> [*He turns and looks at* Rhoda *in blank amazement.*]

Bargus.

[*To* Mrs. Boyle-Chewton.] He doesn't like it. I can see he doesn't like it. Shall we, for the present — that is, temporarily, you know — a year or two — yield to him !

Mrs. Boyle-Chewton.

Doesn't like it! When did I receive sympathy from my brother Dudley? Mr. Bargus, we will take the air before returning to the heated rooms. Your arm. Rhoda, please follow.

[*She takes* Bargus's *arm, and leads him across to the window; as he passes* Rhoda *he gives her a piteous look; his mouth moves without any sound, and he shakes his head violently. She turns from him contemptuously. The three disappear into the garden, leaving* Dudley, *with his hands in his pockets, transfixed.*]

Dudley.

Good gracious! The infant has grown out of all knowledge. Confound it! Edith ought to have known better. I'll go up to the club and drop a line to Bargus. If the babe doesn't listen to reason I'll choke him with his own coral.

A Servant *enters.*

Servant.

Here is Mr. Silchester, my lady.

Dudley.

Eh?

Lady Vivash *enters; her manner is now quite composed, but her step is heavy and slow, and her face pale.*

LADY VIVASH.

Mr. Silchester!

DUDLEY

Lady Vivash!

LADY VIVASH.

Will you find Sylvia for me? I think she must be in the garden. Her young American must pay the penalty of being late; I am going to take his sweetheart home.

DUDLEY.

She'll be a little disappointed.

LADY VIVASH.

[*To herself.*] *She* knows her lover will call to-morrow! Disappointed! I could teach her what that means. [*Sinking wearily into a chair.*

DUDLEY.

You look very tired.

LADY VIVASH.

The rooms are hot — or cold — or something. Find Sylvia, and let me go.

[*The* SERVANT *has drawn the curtains over the window and retired.* DUDLEY *is going into the garden.*]

LADY VIVASH.

[*Calling.*] Dudley! Isn't it curious about — no Mr. Lyster?

DUDLEY.

It is quite a mystery. You saw his letter?

LADY VIVASH.

I didn't scrutinize it. I suppose it *was* his handwriting?

DUDLEY.

I suppose so. I have it with me. [*Taking the letter from his pocket and reading.*] "Next Wednesday night at a party at Lord Gillingham's." They don't know him. Do you recognize the writing?

LADY VIVASH.

Lend me the letter; I'll glance at it when I get home — if I have time.

DUDLEY.

Certainly. [*Giving her the letter; her hand trembling as she takes it.*] I shall call at his hotel to-morrow.

LADY VIVASH.

You — you are not looking for Sylvia.

DUDLEY.

I beg your pardon.

[*He goes out through the curtains into the garden.*]

LADY VIVASH.

[*Looking at the letter.*] The handwriting! Know it! O Philip! you taught it to me too well years ago! "At Lord Gillingham's." He must have written that name for some other. I'll find out to-morrow —early to-morrow. [*She folds the letter, looks around, then touches her lips with the paper and slips it into her bodice.*] Where is Sylvia? Why doesn't she come? I can't endure this place now. [*She crosses to the curtains and holds them open, looking up.*] How bright! It was moonlight when I sent him away from me. What a mockery it is to-night!

> [*She goes through the curtains as* LADY GILLINGHAM *enters with* IRA LEE. *At the same moment the* SERVANT *crosses the room.*]

LADY GILLINGHAM.

[*To the* SERVANT.] Lady Vivash has not gone, Spencer?

SERVANT.

I believe not, my lady. [*The* SERVANT *goes out.*

LADY GILLINGHAM.

[*To* LEE.] I am sure Lady Vivash is most anxious to see you. She must be in the rooms. Wait here; I'll find her and bring her to you.

LEE.

You are very kind to me, Lady Gillingham.

LADY GILLINGHAM.

I am afraid I am. Ah, Mr. Lee, lovers are too troublesome.

LEE.

[*Taking her hand and bending over it.*] Ah, Lady Gillingham, women are too beautiful. [LADY GILLINGHAM *smiles, and goes out.*] Wait here! wait here! to be approved of — or otherwise. To have every gray hair in my head counted, every furrow in my face measured, every pound in the bank weighed. After all, a man on the right side of forty isn't so very old — not so very old. I am only old for Sylvia. Ah, if they don't inspect me quickly I shall be an octogenarian. [*His foot touches a little plain gold bracelet which is lying upon the tiger-skin before the fireplace.*] What's that? [*Picking it up carelessly.*] A bracelet. [*He is about to place it on the mantelpiece when he catches sight of an inscription upon it.*] Great Heaven! [*Reading the inscription.*] "Philip Lyster to Mary Norbury. For ever and ever."

[*The curtains are pushed aside, and* LADY VIVASH *enters, clasping her wrists.*]

LADY VIVASH.

My bracelet! I have lost my bracelet! [*He rises; they come face to face.*] Mr. Lyster!

LEE.

[*Quietly handing the bracelet.*] Are you looking for this? I found it on the ground there.

LADY VIVASH.

[*Taking the bracelet from him, and trying to command herself.*] Thank you. Mr. Silchester mentioned to me that you were thinking of returning to England after — rather a long absence. [*Offering her hand.*] How do you do? [*He takes her hand respectfully, and bows without speaking.*] I did ask about you early in the evening when I first came, but poor Lord Gillingham was more than usually oblivious. He is much changed. We are all very, very much changed.

LEE.

Naturally.

LADY VIVASH.

[*Lightly.*] I think I should have known you anywhere. You wouldn't, of course, have recognized me if I — if I had not — if —

LEE.

Oh, yes — don't mistake me — I should, indeed.

[*Their eyes meet ; she hangs her head and moves a step or two from him.*]

LADY VIVASH.

Old friends ought to feel interested in one another. Have you prospered abroad? Are you — unmarried?

LEE.

Yes; I am unmarried.

LADY VIVASH.

[*Stifling a cry.*] Oh!

LEE.

Yes, old friends ought to feel interested in one another. Pardon me — have you prospered at home? Are you — unmarried?

LADY VIVASH.

Don't you know?

LEE.

Know what?

LADY VIVASH.

Of my marriage — after — you — left England?

LEE.

No. How soon after I left England?

LADY VIVASH.

O Philip! Ah, don't think more hardly of me than you can help. I was mad — I didn't know what I was doing. Heaven pitied me, and gave me strength to do my duty; but you, a man, can't think leniently. I know — I know.

> [*She covers her eyes with her hands. He turns from her respectfully. The curtains move, and* RHODA *is about to enter; seeing* LADY VIVASH, *she stops quickly, and draws back, listening, closing the curtains carefully.*]

LEE.

[*After a pause.*] You have not told me — how soon after I left England.

Lady Vivash.

I can't — I daren't. If you had come back it would have been different. Why didn't you come back?

Lee.

Why? Ha! Because I was a foolish, sentimental lad, with an ideal which you had shattered. Because I was smarting under the charges of unfaithfulness you had brought against me.

Lady Vivash.

False charges; they were false, and I knew it. I tortured you with doubts and accusations for the sake of hearing you tell me how deeply you loved me. I quarrelled for the luxury of reconciliation — stabbed for the sake of healing! And you couldn't comprehend a woman's nature.

Lee.

No; because I forgot that it was the patrician ladies who cried *"Habet"* loudest at the Roman circus. I discovered that you had meant to torture me in play, and I left you, from that moment never to glance back. I made a new man of myself, shunning all chances of hearing of you or reading of you, never letting myself even wonder about you. I was unmanly, you say? Well, men have their excuses even for that — if women are unwomanly.

Lady Vivash.

But now — we are older, wiser.

LEE.

Now! Oh, it can't matter to either of us *now*.

LADY VIVASH.

Not *matter!* Philip, you don't know me. Listen — you must. If you wish it, you shall never see me again after to-night — to-night, the cross-road of our later life. But hear me before we part! While you were shutting your heart upon me in some far-away spot, *my* heart was bleeding for you; my eyes ever looking, my ears ever listening for you!

LEE.

Hush!

LADY VIVASH.

I shock you. A married woman! Yes — but one cruelly treated by her husband. A generous husband might have taught me to forget; as it was, my love for you was the light I burnt to keep me from stumbling. A little child came; to hush it to sleep I cried by its cradle the story of my love for you. I prayed for you night and morning; perhaps my prayers have kept you out of danger!

LEE.

Hush, Mary!

LADY VIVASH.

[*Under her breath.*] What have I said?

LEE.

[*Taking her hand firmly.*] You have said
rightly — this is the cross-road of our lives, and
we part. Good-by !

LADY VIVASH.

Oh !

LEE.

It must be. Because, Mary, both of us are not
free.

LADY VIVASH.

Not free ! Not free ! Ah, I haven't told you,
Philip ! Yes, I *was* married — wretchedly married ; but now it is past. I am — I am alone
again !   [*She totters towards him ; he recoils.*

LEE.

Mary !   .

[LORD *and* LADY GILLINGHAM *enter with*
SYLVIA, *who runs down with a glad cry.*

LADY VIVASH.

[*Hysterically.*] Sylvia !

SYLVIA.

Oh, I am so glad !

LADY VIVASH.

Glad !

SYLVIA.

That you know each other.

LADY VIVASH.

Know — whom ?

SYLVIA.

Mamma dear ! [*Pointing to* LEE.] Mr. Ira Lee !

[LEE *staggers back with a cry.* LADY VI-
VASH *stands for a moment as if turned
to stone ; then* DUDLEY, *who has entered
from the garden, comes quickly to her,
and catches her as she is falling.* RHODA,
MRS. BOYLE-CHEWTON, *and* MR. BARGUS
*appear in the window as the curtain
descends.*]

END OF THE SECOND ACT.

THE THIRD ACT.

The scene is the library at Mrs. Boyle-Chewton's, *as in the First Act, the morning after* Lady Gillingham's *party.*

Mrs. Boyle-Chewton *enters from the garden, with a bundle of flowers, which she surveys sentimentally.*

Mrs. Boyle-Chewton.
Flowers! I feel I have been a little oblivious of the beauty of flowers. This morning I seem to have learnt their language. That little bunch is for me, and that little bunch is for Clarence.

Sylvia *enters in a pretty morning-dress and garden-hat.*

Sylvia.
Good-morning!

Mrs. Boyle-Chewton.
How is mamma?

SYLVIA.

Oh, almost quite well, and laughing at herself for giving way to the heat last night.

MRS. BOYLE-CHEWTON.

The heat! Then she hasn't told you of the strange — [*Stopping in confusion.*] Ah'm!

SYLVIA.

Not told me — what, dear Mrs. Chewton?

MRS. BOYLE-CHEWTON.

Of — of the strange sensations in her head. [*To herself.*] I forgot that Rhoda learnt the affair by accident, and that I am supposed to know nothing.

[*She sits, arranging the flowers as* RHODA *enters.*]

RHODA.

[*Sulkily.*] Good-morning.

SYLVIA.

Good-morning.

MRS. BOYLE-CHEWTON.

[*Childishly.*] Good-morning, little one.

RHODA.

[*Angrily to herself.*] Oh! when I was a child I was treated like a woman; now I seem to have suddenly become a baby!

[*She sits at the table, and takes up a newspaper;* MRS. BOYLE-CHEWTON *hums a
tune, at which* RHODA *stamps her foot
and clutches the paper in a rage.* SYL-
VIA *looks from one to the other, quite
mystified.*]

RHODA.

Mamma! [*To herself.*] Mamma never could
sing.

[MRS. BOYLE-CHEWTON *continues humming
unconsciously.*]

SYLVIA.

[*Quietly to* RHODA.] Rhoda dear, I am afraid
I lost my temper last night, and was very unkind.
Will you forgive me?

RHODA.

Oh, certainly — of course!

SYLVIA.

Thank you. And now I'll say what I ought to
have said when you told me about Mr. Bargus. I
congratulate you with all my heart!

RHODA.

[*Looking towards her mother.*] Hush! Be quiet!

SYLVIA.

[*Surprised.*] Don't you want me to congratulate
you?

RHODA.

[*Under her breath.*] No — no — there's nothing to congratulate me upon. I mean — I — I — How is Lady Vivash this morning?

SYLVIA.

Quite well; it was only the heat of the room.

RHODA.

The heat of the room! Then you don't know —

MRS. BOYLE-CHEWTON.

[*Who is now listening.*] Hush, Rhoda!

SYLVIA.

Don't know — what?

RHODA.

Oh, nothing!

SYLVIA.

[*Looking from one to the other.*] Oh, I am afraid there is something you are keeping from me! You don't think mamma is really ill, do you? You would tell me if you thought so!

MRS. BOYLE-CHEWTON.

Of course! Lady Vivash is in most excellent health. Why, look at her!

[LADY VIVASH *enters; her face is pale, but otherwise she is quite herself.*]

LADY VIVASH.

Good-morning.

RHODA *and* MRS. BOYLE-CHEWTON.

Good-morning!

MRS. BOYLE-CHEWTON.

We are so glad you are better, Mary.

LADY VIVASH.

Thank you.   Till last night I had not fainted for years.   It was very foolish of me.   Did you — did you feel the heat?

MRS. BOYLE-CHEWTON.

No; not particularly.

LADY VIVASH.

Did you, Rhoda?

RHODA.

[*With meaning, eying* LADY VIVASH.]   No.   I was outside the room in which you fainted — outside, by the window.

LADY VIVASH.

By the window?   Oh, of course; it was cooler there!

RHODA.

Yes; much cooler.

LADY VIVASH.

[*To herself.*] She couldn't have heard!

SYLVIA.

[*To* LADY VIVASH.] Mamma, dear, come into the garden, and watch for Mr. Lee.

LADY VIVASH.

[*Starting.*] Mr. Lee!

SYLVIA.

He said he would be here very early in the morning. He was so anxious about you. Do come!

LADY VIVASH.

For a few minutes, darling; I must be very busy to-day. [*To* MRS. BOYLE-CHEWTON, *as* SYLVIA *runs up to the window.*] Edith, dear, what with Sylvia's return, and — and the party last night — and — and one thing and another, I have neglected the work which is so near to your heart and mine. But my mind shall never wander again, dear. Forgive me, and let us make up for lost time to-day.

MRS. BOYLE-CHEWTON.

[*Bashfully.*] Um. *I* don't feel very much in-clined for work to-day.

LADY VIVASH.

You — not inclined to work!

MRS. BOYLE-CHEWTON.

No.

LADY VIVASH.

But we have a Finance Committee at four o'clock.

MRS. BOYLE-CHEWTON.

Oh, bother the Finance Committee !

LADY VIVASH.

Edith !

DUDLEY *enters quickly.*

DUDLEY.

Good-morning.   I am a little early, Edith — but the fact is —

MRS. BOYLE-CHEWTON.

You are fortunate.   By being early you stand a chance of meeting Clarence — Mr. Bargus.   I'm on the lookout for him.

[*Going to the window and looking out.*

DUDLEY.

[*To himself.*]   Oh, if she only knew that the infant is now on the premises, waiting to tell her of the dreadful mistake he has made !   Phew ! and there she is — on the lookout for him.   How can I break it ?   [LADY VIVASH *comes to* DUDLEY's *side.*

LADY VIVASH.

[*Softly to him.*]   Dudley.

DUDLEY.

Are you better?

LADY VIVASH.

Quite well. Dudley, Ira Lee — Philip Lyster
— is coming here this morning. I have thought
over everything, and I have decided. Dudley, the
knowledge that he was once my lover must be
kept from Sylvia.

DUDLEY.

But, my dear Mary —

LADY VIVASH.

Oh, where would be the good? It was years
and years ago, and is done with. The secret is
quite our own. She loves him dearly; I know him
to be a good man. Would you set me, her mother,
up between them? Oh, it would be cruel!

DUDLEY.

But is he sure his old affection is quite extinct,
with a decent, respectable, and heavy monument
upon it?

LADY VIVASH.

Sure! My Sylvia is *what I was* — of course he
loves her.

DUDLEY.

And you, Mary — Sylvia's mother?

[*She starts and trembles, and her eyes droop
for a moment.*]

LADY VIVASH.

I love only Sylvia.

[*She joins* SYLVIA *at the window.*

MRS. BOYLE-CHEWTON.

[*Looking at the clock.*] Rhoda, didn't Mr. Bargus say he would be here at ten o'clock ?

DUDLEY.

[*Nervously.*]   Oh, my dear Edith, that reminds
me.   Ah — um — Mr. Bargus *is* here.

MRS. BOYLE-CHEWTON.

Here ! and I not informed !

DUDLEY.

Well, the fact is, my dear Edith, he — he's sitting
in the Committee Room.

MRS. BOYLE-CHEWTON.

Sitting in the Committee Room !   He can't be a
committee all by himself.

DUDLEY.

No ; he realizes that.   He will be all right in a
minute.

MRS. BOYLE-CHEWTON.

He is not well !   I see it in your expression ;
Mr. Bargus is indisposed !

DUDLEY.

Well — yes — that's it. Bargus is a little indisposed.

MRS. BOYLE-CHEWTON.

Oh!

DUDLEY.

He came to me very early this morning, before I was up, in fact, to — to make some explanations. And having had a bad night he asked me to bring him along.

MRS. BOYLE-CHEWTON.

A bad night! Oh, dear! oh, dear!

[*She rings the bell.*

DUDLEY.

Stop! Edith! I think — I fancy he wishes to see you alone.

MRS. BOYLE-CHEWTON.

Of course he does. But I must present him to Mary in his proper light. Mary!

DUDLEY.

No, no! No, no! I've something to tell you!

MRS. BOYLE-CHEWTON.

I will have no secrets. Mr. Bargus and I have nothing to be ashamed of.

DUDLEY.

Yes, you have — I mean, he has. Oh, wait! wait!

MRS. BOYLE-CHEWTON.

Wait! I ought to have told Mary the first thing this morning. Mary!

DUDLEY.

Oh, here it goes!

MRS. BOYLE-CHEWTON.

Mary, you will be surprised to hear that Mr. Bargus and I are engaged to be married.

LADY VIVASH.

Edith!

SYLVIA.

O Rhoda!

[RHODA *turns away with a cry of rage.*

MRS. BOYLE-CHEWTON.

It will take Mr. Bargus's eloquent tongue to tell you our reasons for changing our condition. But the Cause, dear Mary, the great Cause shall not suffer.

PETCH *enters.*

MRS. BOYLE-CHEWTON.

Petch, Mr. Bargus is in the Committee Room — beg him to come here.   [PETCH *goes out.*

DUDLEY.

[*To himself.*] Poor devil! What a muddle I've made of it!

LADY VIVASH.

My dear Edith! [*Kissing her.*] I hope you
will be very happy.

SYLVIA.

And so do I, dear Mrs. Chewton, indeed. O
Rhoda has been having such fun with me!

RHODA.

[*Angrily.*] Oh!

SYLVIA.

Yes; Rhoda told me last night that Mr. Bargus —

RHODA.

[*Furiously.*] Miss Vivash!
    [RHODA *goes out into the garden as* PETCH
      enters.]

PETCH.

Mr. Bargus!
    [BARGUS *enters ; he is pale and dejected, with*
      a wild look in his eyes, and his appear-
      ance generally disordered. PETCH *goes*
      out.]

BARGUS.

Oh, good-morning!

LADY VIVASH.

Mr. Bargus, I have just heard some news which
gives me very great pleasure. Let me be among
the first to congratulate you warmly.
              [*She takes his hand.*

BARGUS.

[*Weakly.*]   Oh!

LADY VIVASH.

Come, Sylvia, dear.

[LADY VIVASH *and* SYLVIA *go out by the window.*]

BARGUS.

Mr. Silchester, why have you done this?

DUDLEY.

I'm desperately sorry — upon my soul I am.

MRS. BOYLE-CHEWTON.

[*To* BARGUS.]   They tell me you are not well.
[BARGUS *shakes his head helplessly ; she gives him the bunch of flowers.*]   Those are for you.

[*He takes them, and sinks into a chair; she regarding him fondly.*]

BARGUS.

[*Appealingly.*]   Mr. Silchester.

DUDLEY.

My dear Edith, it is of no use to beat about the
bush any farther.   The fact is, Mr. Bargus, who
mistrusts his own strength of mind, has begged me
to be his spokesman.   Edith, Mr. Bargus continues
to entertain the highest admiration, the most pro-
found respect for you, but — but —

Mrs. Boyle-Chewton.

But! but what, Dudley?

Dudley.

But he feels it due to himself and to you to say
that the events of last night were based upon an
entire misunderstanding.

Mrs. Boyle-Chewton.

The events of last night?

Dudley.

The — the proposal of marriage.

Mrs. Boyle-Chewton.

The proposal of marriage! Mr. Bargus desires
to withdraw it?

Dudley.

Well — he places himself entirely in your hands.
In point of fact, dear Edith, Mr. Bargus intended
to propose for Rhoda; his expressions were am-
biguous, and he thought he was doing so when he
wasn't. Phew! I hope I make myself perfectly
clear.

Mrs. Boyle-Chewton.

[*After a slight pause.*] Quite — quite. So far
as I am concerned the matter has been a momen-
tary distraction, nothing more. For Rhoda? Oh,
yes; just so. Dudley, thank Mr. Bargus for his
promptness. These mistakes are better corrected
at the moment. It — it is an amusing error.
[*Giving way.*] Oh, what a fool I've been!

[*She sinks into a chair and sobs violently.*
BARGUS *rises, and* DUDLEY *energetically
waves him towards the door.*]

DUDLEY.

[*Under his breath to* BARGUS.] Go away; don't
say anything! Get out!

BARGUS.

Oh, I should like to say before I go that Mrs.
Boyle-Chewton's magnanimous behavior under the
present distressing circumstances increases my
admiration for the generosity of her disposition.
She is a noble woman.

DUDLEY.

Get out!

BARGUS.

Many plans of atonement have suggested themselves to me during the lonely hours of an entirely
sleepless night. One of them was to place all my
worldly possessions at Mrs. Boyle-Chewton's dis-
posal for charitable distribution. In such a case I
should desire the Asylum for Idiots to participate
largely.

MRS. BOYLE-CHEWTON.

[*Sobbing.*] Oh—h—h—h—!

DUDLEY.

Get out!

BARGUS.

I am about to act on your suggestion. Good-day. Er—um, I desire to say, finally, that at half-past five this morning I arrived at the conclusion that I am peculiarly unfitted for public life. To-morrow I apply for the stewardship of the Chiltern Hundreds. [DUDLEY *moves towards the bell.*] Thank you, I'll let myself out. Mr. Silchester, I shall remain in town until Tuesday, in case you should desire to pursue the matter to a dreadful issue. Good-morning! [*He goes out quietly.*

MRS. BOYLE-CHEWTON.

O Dudley, take me to my room! I shall never hold up my head again.

DUDLEY.

Yes, you will — to-morrow.

MRS. BOYLE-CHEWTON.

I've been false to my principles!

DUDLEY.

Well, well, everybody is. You can get some new ones.

MRS. BOYLE-CHEWTON.

There's something wrong with us women! With all our struggles for equality, we are so weak, so incomplete!

DUDLEY.

Of course you are! You'll never make one boc
a pair if you polish it till doomsday!

[*He takes her out as* SYLVIA'*s voice is hear*
outside.]

SYLVIA.

[*Appearing outside window.*] Remain there,
mamma! I'll fetch your hat and a shawl. [*Run-*
ning across to the door.] I wish he would make
haste!

[*She runs out at the door as* RHODA *enters*
by the window, watching her.]

RHODA.

She is not to know, then! Her little butterfly
wings are not to be fluttered even with the knowledge that her sweetheart's love is very second-
hand. Why should everything be so smooth for
her and so rough for me? Why shouldn't I tell
her the truth?

SYLVIA *re-enters, carrying a hat and shawl.*

RHODA.

[*Intercepting her.*] Sylvia!

SYLVIA.

I — I must hurry with these to mamma.

RHODA.

Look here — I want to speak to you. Don't you
think it is time that you made people regard you

as something better than a doll ? Do you think it
is just that your mother and your friends should
keep you ignorant of what concerns you more than
anybody in the world ?

SYLVIA.

I am very happy. A great many things I dare
say I don't know. If people love me or like me
that's all I *want* to know.

RHODA.

But don't you want to know everything concerning the people *you* love ? Say, for instance, the
man you love ?

SYLVIA.

Are you speaking of Mr. Ira Lee ?

RHODA.

Who is Mr. Ira Lee ?

SYLVIA.

Mr. Philip Lyster. He bears two names, both
good and honorable.

RHODA.

You do know, then — all about him !

SYLVIA.

All about him !

RHODA.

[*Contemptuously.*] I see. You are more a woman than I thought you. Your cloak, Sylvia, is

not so much gossamer as good waterproof. They
have taught you, I suppose, that you ought to be
well satisfied with second-hand love — when the
lover is a poet.

SYLVIA.

What — what do you mean?

RHODA.

Your mother is waiting for her hat and shawl.

SYLVIA.

Rhoda — tell me!

RHODA.

There's nothing more to tell. You know that
Mr. Lee Lyster had a sweetheart years ago; you
know, I presume, who the lady was; *voilà tout!* I
thought you were too confiding or I shouldn't have
bothered you.

[SYLVIA *puts the hat and shawl upon the
writing-table tremblingly.*]

SYLVIA.

You — you are mistaken. They have told me
nothing.   Rhoda — what is it?

RHODA.

Oh, *I'd* rather not tell you!

SYLVIA.

You must — now.   What is it?

RHODA.

Promise to forget that it came from me if I *do*
tell you — never to mention my name.

SYLVIA.

Yes, yes; I promise.

[LADY VIVASH *appears at window.*

SYLVIA.

Be quick! A sweetheart, years ago — who was
she?

RHODA.

I suppose the past tense applies — she is not
dead, you know. [LADY VIVASH *enters the room.*

SYLVIA.

Far away, then?

RHODA.

No, indeed.

SYLVIA.

Not near us — in our own country?

RHODA.

Quite in our own country — very near us.

SYLVIA.

Who is she?

[LADY VIVASH *utters a suppressed cry.*

RHODA.

I wonder you don't guess — Lady Vivash.

SYLVIA.

Oh, no!

LADY VIVASH.

Sylvia!

SYLVIA.

Mother!

[LADY VIVASH *clasps* SYLVIA *in her arms;
but the girl slips from her, and falls on
her knees at her mother's feet, burying
her face in her hands.*]

LADY VIVASH.

[*To* RHODA.] Leave me with my child, please.
[RHODA *takes a step or two, and moves her lips as
if trying to speak ; but her eyes meet* LADY VIVASH'S,
*her head droops, and she goes slowly and silently
through the window and out of sight.*] Gossamer,
look at me. [*She stoops and gently raises* SYLVIA.]
Look at me, dear — your mother.

SYLVIA.

[*In a whisper.*] Is it true?

[LADY VIVASH *shrinks a little, then stands
with her face averted, holding* SYLVIA'S
hand.]

LADY VIVASH.

Yes. [SYLVIA *goes back with a faint cry; but*
LADY VIVASH *catches her in her arms, and kisses
her passionately.*] Oh, listen, listen, listen! It is
strange, but nothing else. There is no need for
you to give even a second thought to a foolish ac-

cident — the last weak thread in the remnant of
the old past. Sylvia! Sylvia!

[SYLVIA *sinks into a chair, staring forward
vacantly.*]

SYLVIA.

Mother!

[LADY VIVASH *kneels to* SYLVIA, *taking her
hands, and clasping them tremblingly.*]

LADY VIVASH.

O my darling, my darling! Ah, don't look
like that! There is nothing in this — accident
that should trouble you. He is yours, heart and
soul. Years and years ago he may have had a
passing fancy; but the girl he l — liked is now
a rigid, prosaic, strong-minded creature whom some
men laugh and jeer at. You'll make me believe
I've wronged you! Kiss me — your poor mother
— your poor mother, who would let you trample
on her to save you a moment's pain! My darling!
My darling!

SYLVIA.

I haven't heard the name of your boy-lover till
now. [*In a dream.*] Philip Lyster — Philip
Lyster.

LADY VIVASH.

You're right — he was only a boy-lover. And
love to a lad is a toy, nothing more; when he is
tired of it he breaks it and flings it away. *You*
are loved by a man!

SYLVIA.

I see the reason he changed his life and his name — to try to forget everything — himself — his love.

LADY VIVASH.

And he *did* forget! he *did* forget!

SYLVIA.

Yes — but, mother dear, *you* have not forgotten!

LADY VIVASH.

[*Rising aghast.*] Sylvia!

SYLVIA.

Do you think I don't remember the story of your love as you told it to me one day when you were in trouble, when you said to me, "Sylvia, a woman's first love is her religion." Ah, I remember, I remember — so well.

LADY VIVASH.

[*Sinking into a chair.*] Oh my child! my child!

SYLVIA.

[*Going to* LADY VIVASH.] Forgive me, mother. It is I who have brought trouble upon you, not you upon me. [*Kneeling at her feet,* LADY VIVASH *sobs bitterly.*] Hush, mother dear! mother dear! I was selfish ever to think of leaving you. We'll never part, dear; we'll never part.

LADY VIVASH.

[*In agony.*] Oh, what have I done to you!
What have I done to you! What have I done
to you!

DUDLEY *enters.*

LADY VIVASH.

[*Advancing to meet* DUDLEY.] Dudley.

DUDLEY.

Here is Philip, Mary

LADY VIVASH.

[*Under her breath.*] Philip!

> [*The two women look at each other.* SYLVIA
> *walks slowly to* LADY VIVASH, *kisses her,*
> *and goes softly out at the window.*]

DUDLEY.

Mary, Sylvia knows?

> [LADY VIVASH *bows her head.*

LADY VIVASH.

[*With an effort.*] Tell him to come to me.

> [DUDLEY *goes to the door and beckons to*
> LEE, *then goes and stands outside the*
> *window, as* LEE *enters.*]

LEE.

Lady Vivash.

LADY VIVASH.

She knows. My child knows!

LEE.

Oh!

LADY VIVASH.

Help me! Help me!

LEE.

Tell me how. Tell me.

LADY VIVASH.

You *do* love her truly? [*Entreatingly.*] You
do, you do?

LEE.

I do.

LADY VIVASH.

Then by your love for that girl who has never
known an unhappy moment until to-day; out of
pity for the wretched woman who wounded you
years ago —

LEE.

Ah, Mary, hush! —

LADY VIVASH.

Yes, out of compassion for me, do your utmost
to remove the sorrow which has fallen upon my
child. [LEE *makes a despairing gesture.*] Ah,
don't hesitate. Try, try to comprehend the position in which I am. It is no longer mother and
daughter with Sylvia and myself; it is woman and
woman. Ah, don't hesitate!

LEE.

What — what do you bid me do?

[*Burying his face in his hands.*

LADY VIVASH.

Convince her that your love for her is the real love of your life; declare to her that your old boyish infatuation was nothing but a flame which you smothered with a stamp of your foot. You must win back her trust and confidence. You must make her happy again. You hear me — you *must* — you *must*.

LEE.

And then, Lady Vivash? What then? Is there no future to reckon for? Are there no ghosts to rise, no seeds of distrust to break their husks, spring up, and bear fruit? What of the future?

LADY VIVASH.

The future! Listen, Philip Lyster. I love my child. She is all I live for now. But if I could know she was happy, I could be content to live out the rest of my life away from her; never to disturb her; never to break in upon her peace; never by sight of my face to make her think.

LEE.

O Lady Vivash!

LADY VIVASH.

You understand what I mean? If you can make her happy, I will go away from you both.

The man she loves is more to a girl than the mother who loves her, and I will pay a mother's penalty; a little heavier than most mothers pay — but — I will pay it to the full. [*Faintly clutching at the back of a chair, then recovering herself, and holding out her hand to* LEE.] Philip Lyster, won't you help me ?

LEE.

[*Looking at her distractedly and irresolutely, then taking her hand.*] Yes, I *will* help you.

LADY VIVASH.

Ah, you will do your utmost ?

LEE.

I will do my utmost. I promise.

LADY VIVASH.

Oh, I thank you !
LEE.

Hush ! hush !
LADY VIVASH.

Yes, I thank you. I bless you. May I go and find Sylvia now ?
LEE.

Yes, yes.
LADY VIVASH.

Wait, then, wait. [*Going slowly to the window, and catching at the curtain, she sees the bracelet on her wrist ; then turning to look at* LEE, *who stands staring forward, she removes the bracelet, and creeps towards him.*] The bracelet.

> [LEE *looks up with a start, and takes the bracelet which she hands him, with averted face, then she goes out.*]

LEE.

[*Seeing* DUDLEY *outside.*] Dudley! [DUDLEY *approaches.*] Give me your hand. [*They grip hands.*] Old friend, say good-by to me.

DUDLEY.

Philip! What are you going to do?

LEE.

My utmost to heal the sorrow I have brought upon Mary and Sylvia. I have come into their lives to their cost — to *my* cost I will go out of their lives to-day as if I had died at this very hour.

DUDLEY.

Does Mary know?

LEE.

Not yet. Tell her, Dudley, that I have kept my promise — that I have done my utmost.

DUDLEY.

O Philip, is there no way but this?

LEE.

None. You know it, Dudley. Once my shadow is taken from the lives of these two women, there will be light again. I pray to time to do the rest. Time will bless some worthier man than I with Sylvia's sweet companionship, and then the first laugh from Sylvia's lips will wake Mary from her long dream. You will be near them still, Dudley, —always?

DUDLEY.

Always. I am too old a watch-dog to know any voice but Mary's.   [*They shake hands.*

LEE.

God bless you ! This is the only way.

[*Bows his head on* DUDLEY'S *shoulder.*

DUDLEY.

They are coming.

LEE.

[*With emotion.*] Let me see them once more together. Let me see them when they know that I have gone. Tell them.

[LEE *goes out at one window, as* LADY VI-VASH *and* SYLVIA *enter at another, without seeing him.*]

LADY VIVASH.

[*Quietly to* DUDLEY.] Dudley, Philip has something to tell Sylvia which I want her to hear from

his lips alone. Where is he? Let us find him.
Come.   [*Going towards the door.*

DUDLEY.

[*Stopping her.*] Mary — Sylvia.

LADY VIVASH.

Dudley!

DUDLEY.

I have some news to break to you. We shall
see Philip no more. He has gone. [LADY
VIVASH *and* SYLVIA *meet each other's eyes with a
fixed look.*] Mary, Philip asks me to tell you that
he has kept his promise. He has done his utmost.

> [LADY VIVASH *goes to* SYLVIA, *and they
> tenderly embrace.* DUDLEY *goes to the
> window and looks out; then* LEE *re-
> enters silently, looks at the two women,
> grips* DUDLEY'S *hand, and disappears.*]

THE END.

www.ingramcontent.com/pod-product-compliance
Lightning Source LLC
Chambersburg PA
CBHW020408030726
47496CB00007B/2367